CONTROL

THE MYSTERY OF LANDON MILLER BOOK ONE

R. M. GAUTHIER

DEDICATION

There are many people who had a hand in this novel.

To begin with, my family, who always support everything I do. I know how rare this can be.

To my friends, who have read this story and have patiently, or not so patiently, waited 5 years for book 2. Luckily, my fans won't have to wait near that long. Sorry, to my friends.

CONTENTS

CHAPTER 1

My heart pounds against my chest as Haley eases the car down the darkened alleyway. I peer ahead, barely making out what I'm hoping is a valet attendant opening the door to the car in front of us.

Another man stands in the doorway to the building on our right. My heart resumes a normal beat. Haley knew what she was doing all along and I'm chastising myself for not having more faith in her.

I glance at her and see a grin spread across her face, but it only lasts a moment. Then, she pulls the car forward alongside another valet attendant who awaits our arrival. Her expression morphs and becomes deadly serious.

"You remember the rules?" Her eyebrows pinch together as she glares at me.

"Yes."

"Good. Follow them and we'll be fine." Her gaze holds mine prisoner for a few seconds, before she turns forward in her seat, pulls the door handle and steps out of the vehicle.

My heart speeds up again as I do a mental check of the rules. A tremor runs through me when I swing my door open and a man offers me his hand. His lips are moving but I'm too busy repeating the list of rules in my head to hear what he is saying. I place my hand in his, step out of the car and wait for Haley.

"Follow me," she says, her voice clipped, as she walks towards the door.

Her tone stuns me and the need to say something about it needles me, but I don't because the *rules* forbid talking. Instead, I fall into step behind her.

She glances at the doorman who swings the door to the building open as he ogles her, which is not unusual. Haley's a beautiful woman and garners plenty of attention. She's a tall, blonde with the most piercing blue eyes. She comes from a privileged background, which gives her a sense of arrogance enough to be confident but not enough to make her annoying. I love this woman as if she were my own sister.

I, on the other hand, stand at a whopping five foot-four with long brown, shaggy hair, which rarely does as expected. Big, round brown mud colored eyes. At least I have a straight nose, though it could be a bit smaller. Not that I have a huge nose per-se—but if I'm being completely honest—it's easy to find faults in myself. As for my wardrobe—well, as Haley has so eloquently stated on several occasions—my clothes make me look forty-five instead of twenty-five. Fashion has never been a priority for me, unlike Haley who is the owner of a designer company.

Haley and I have been best friends since we were five years old. She's always been a huge part of my life. She is the one person in the world I can tell anything to and know she will never steer me wrong. Somehow she has a way of fixing things.

"Good evening, Miss Rose."

"Good evening, Riley," Haley responds, curtly.

My gaze falls to the ground because that's another *rule* —don't make eye contact with anyone.

We walk into the building and the heavy steel door slams shut behind us causing my heart to drop into my stomach. I'm consumed by fear and excitement waiting for further instructions.

The room is silent giving no indication of the type of establishment we're in. While the desire to glance around is strong, instead I keep my gaze fixed to the floor.

Another *rule*—eyes down unless permission is granted to look around freely.

Haley walks forward a couple of steps and I quickly follow. Abruptly, she stops causing me to almost crash into her. She spins around coming face-to-face with me.

"Sit." Her tone is clipped, once again.

There's a couch along the wall next to us, so I take the few steps over to it and sit. Haley eases into the seat beside me.

"You may look around this room." Her tone is that of a mother reprimanding a young child.

I lift my head and glance around. The room is nothing

special containing simple furnishings of a black leather couch and two red armchairs. The color arrangement is strange—red and black. The bottom half of the room is black, and the top half of the room is red—blood red. As I wonder who the designer is Haley's voice pulls me from my thoughts.

"All right, Shaw. Game faces on. No laughing, smiling, or giggling. Keep the look you have on your face now throughout the night, unless I give you permission other-wise. All right?" She is deadly serious and I, a little afraid.

Just what the hell is this place?

"Okay." I sound more like a petulant child then the adult I claim to be.

"I mean it. This is extremely important." She gives me a pleading look.

"Fine. I'll follow all your rules. Promise." I tap two fingers over my heart, then hold them in the air.

"Okay. Here we go." She whispers.

Here we go! Here we go where?

The sound of a door opening has my gaze quickly falling to the floor. Footsteps echoing on the tiles get louder and closer. Expensive Italian loafers come into my line of vision letting me know the person standing in front of us is male. My heart rate picks up as my brain scrambles through many thoughts.

"Miss Rose, how have you been?" the gentleman asks with false enthusiasm laced in his tone.

"Great, Leroy. And yourself?" Haley replies.

It's a struggle keeping my eyes on the floor as I strain not to sneak a peek.

"Good. Things have been good. Busy, of course. Now, who's your friend?" he inquires.

"Leroy, this is Alexandria. You may look up, Alexandria," Haley snarls with the same cold tone she's been using since our arrival.

Peeking up, the man standing in front of me is tall—very tall, well-built and glaring right at me. He is a nice-looking man wearing an expensive three-piece suit, his muscles ripple underneath almost bursting out of the material. He has brown curly hair that appears messy, but not quite messy because nothing about this man is out of place. He is very well put together.

The way his glare is assessing me is scary. His presence is all-consuming as he keeps me prisoner in his gaze. He appears to be searching my eyes, for what I have no idea, but I know immediately this is not a man I want to upset in anyway. Something in his eyes tells me to behave—and that's exactly what I plan to do.

"It's nice to meet you, Alexandria. What a lovely name you have." He smiles a genuine smile.

"You may speak." Haley's curt tone and attitude shocks me, once again.

What kind of place is this? More importantly, how the hell did I end up here?

This is what I get for asking for advice. I simply told Haley at lunch the other day that I wanted a little fun and excitement in my life and I end up here.

"Thank you," I reply, keeping my tone as calm as I can muster under the circumstance. I'm terrified, but don't want that revealed.

Leroy quickly turns his attention to Haley.

"What will it be tonight, Miss Rose?" he inquires.

"Just the usual. I'll only be looking around tonight. Thank you," Haley answers calmly, with her natural voice.

"You won't need a room tonight?" Leroy inquires, as he glances my way.

A room? What the hell does that mean? Shocked by his question my gaze hits the floor as I try to figure out what the hell is going on and keep a straight face.

"Not this time Leroy, but thank you for offering," she replies.

"Anytime. If you change your mind, come find me." He strolls over to the other side of the room.

I take a quick peek at him while his back is to us. He pushes a button on the wall and part of the wall slides out, it's about the size of a filing cabinet drawer. He reaches in and pulls something out, then turns around and makes his way back to us holding a file in his hand.

I drop my gaze to the floor and twist my hands together in my lap. My mind is in a frenzy wondering where we are and what goes on here.

"Here's your card," Leroy says.

I assume he hands something to Haley because her arm extends towards him.

"I'll see you at the end of your visit. Have an excellent time." His voice is amused, and I grow even more nervous.

Haley stands up from the couch.

"Thank you, Leroy. For everything. I know it was short notice and I'm happy you could accommodate me," she expresses with a tone she rarely uses—grateful. What she's grateful for is not clear, but I'm hoping it'll be revealed soon.

"No problem. Anything for you, Miss Rose. You've been a wonderful customer and we appreciate your business. Have a good evening."

Leroy strolls to the door he entered through and makes his exit.

I peek over at Haley who gives me a chastising glance, and my gaze hits the floor once more.

My whole body is tense, and my heart has yet to settle. If this keeps up much longer I'm certain I'll have a heart attack.

"Come, Alexandria," Haley barks, as she snaps her fingers at me.

The snapping of her fingers is insulting, but I rise from the couch and follow her anyway, even though every instinct in me is screaming to run the other way. I can't because I have to know what this is all about.

Haley's my best friend, she'd never hurt me or put me in harm's way. I have to have faith in her.

Haley strides over to another door in the room. She slides a plastic card—I assume given to her by Leroy— through the slot of a device attached to the wall, sitting on the outside of the door frame.

The door springs open and she strolls through with me in tow. We are now in a room that is about ten-by-ten square feet and completely red in color. The same blood red from the previous room.

"Okay, listen up. You need to remember all the *rules* I

gave you. Don't slip up. Okay?" Haley says, concern laced in her tone.

Her words fluster me because she's typically the strong one of our duo. I've never seen her rattled about anything.

"Yes, I promise. I'll do everything you say. But can you tell me where we are?" I whisper.

"You'll see. Explanations are difficult, seeing is much easier to understand. Now, be the good girl I know you are and follow my rules. I promise you'll love this. One more thing, if for any reason you want to leave. If this gets too much for you, just say the word 'brown'. I'll understand, and we'll go. No questions asked, all right?"

"Okay, 'brown' if I want to leave," I whisper.

"All right—here we go." Haley swipes her card through another slot in the wall and once again a door opens.

She steps into the next room and I follow. Once inside she spins around and like her shadow I do too, taking notice that we're in an elevator.

She presses a button, the doors close and we are on the move. My heart speeds up as the movement of the elevator starts our journey.

Haley believes I'll enjoy this place, and by all the cloak and dagger moves to get in here, I presume we have entered an exclusive club. I'm wondering who we might see and why everything is so secretive. I'm excited and scared, an odd combinations of feelings to have.

As the elevator stops, the doors slide open.

Haley steps out and I mirror her movements except for my view—it's glued to the floor.

CHAPTER 2

*W*e enter a room where soft music is playing in the background and hushed conversations float all around us. Unfortunately, I haven't been granted permission to look around the room, so I can't tell how many people are here, but I can tell by the echo the room is sizable.

Haley doesn't hesitate striding forward with me trailing close behind. We walk quickly through the room—much quicker than my poor feet would like—and out of the corner of my eye I see tables and chairs on either side of us. A few are occupied, but many remain empty.

Curiosity gets the better of me and I take a quick peek to my right, there are several long leather couches placed along the wall. One is occupied by a man in a black suit. He has one leg crossed over his knee and appears relaxed as he sips a drink. There is a woman kneeling on the floor beside his legs with her head bowed to him. He is running his free hand through her hair.

My gaze snaps back to Haley's shoes in front of me and we continue our journey to the back of the room. My mind's in overdrive trying to figure out what I've just witnessed.

We exit through a doorway into a long narrow hallway. We have been walking for longer than I anticipated, and my feet are screaming in protest because of the stilettos I've been forced to endure. Not my typical attire, but my entire outfit was handpicked by Haley, so I really had no other choice in the matter—if I wanted to come. I wish we'd get to where we're going already because my feet can't take much more.

Haley stops at the end of the hall and spins around to face me. I glance up to see her giving me a stern look a reminder to follow her *rules.*

I drop my gaze to the floor and she grabs a hold of my elbow leading me into another room. She tugs me along the wall until we're about half way into the room, then turns us so our backs are to the wall.

"Feel free to look around," she says, her voice cold and crass.

I'm completely consumed by nervous tension—afraid to see where we are. Still, there is another part of me that's intrigued and has a dark desire to know what is happening. An argument breaks out in my mind but it's over quickly and curiosity wins.

I raise my head and glance at my surroundings. The room is crowded with people—both men and women—but most notable is the direction their attention is focused. Everyone is staring at one side of the room.

At first glance it's hard to tell what everyone's focused on and because the crowd is large I can't see over their heads. I shift my weight from one foot to the other attempting to look around a rather tall gentleman blocking my view.

Movement to my left catches my eye and I divert my attention.

Standing in the back corner, away from the crowd is the most exquisite man I've ever seen. He's tall, lean, with the most gorgeous face and striking features. He has a strong angular jaw line, perfect nose, and luscious looking lips. Deep-set eyes with thick, long black lashes that surround the forest green color which stands out against the rest of his characteristics.

He's dressed in a dark suit jacket with a white button up shirt underneath and dark trousers that appear tailor fit hanging off him just right. He's also wearing a pair of expensive Italian loafers. His hair is dark with shades of blond running through it, short enough to be presentable in any situation, but long enough to give off an air of defiance.

My gaze is glued to the man and as hard as I try to make myself look away, I can't. His focus is captured by whatever is happening at the front of the room.

Haley pinches my arm pulling my focus away from the beautiful man. She's caught me staring and is not too pleased. Even though her reaction is evident I can't help sneaking a peek at him again. As I do our gazes lock and I'm hypnotized. I must literally shake my head to look away. Still, I feel his glare on me and it takes all my strength not to reciprocate.

Struggling to keep my attention on the front of the room and the reason we're here, I change my focus to what is happening instead. The man in front of me—who stands over six feet tall—is still blocking my view, so I maneuver sideways a little in order to see.

To say I'm shocked would be an understatement because not twenty feet in front of me is a woman who is chained to the ceiling. The chains run from the ceiling to her wrists, which are encased in cuffs. She's completely naked with only a necklace hanging around her neck.

There's a man standing approximately six feet away from her addressing the crowd, but I'm so stunned by the appearance of the woman that his words sound like a foreign language.

Without warning he flicks his wrist and a whip—which I've just noticed in his hand—whirls through the air and lands on her back. Hard. As it lands, it makes this awful snapping sound making my body shudder as it registers the impact.

My mind goes haywire and I feel the blood drain from my face. My brain is shouting at me to help this woman, but my mouth and body are immovable.

I glance over at Haley, but she has no reaction—nothing at all. Stunned, I glance around the room and not one person moves, not one person says or does anything, there's complete silence in the room, except for the man with the whip. He's saying something to the viewers, but my minds in shock and can't comprehend his actual words.

Abruptly, he flicks his wrist again. This time the whip lands on her ass with another loud snap.

I jump a little following the impact. My mind is still yelling as my body goes rigid. I believe I may pass out.

But, one question is on repeat in my mind—*why is nobody stopping him?*

As my mind races, I glance at the woman's face and realize two things simultaneously, she isn't screaming, and she hasn't moved a muscle.

What does that mean? Is she even alive?

I twist my head around the man in front of me to get a better view and study her facial expression. To my relief, she is very much alive. *How can she just stand there? Surely, that had to hurt?* But still, there's no movement or noise from her. Perhaps it's an illusion. Maybe he's a magician or something.

One more loud snap and my mind comes rushing back to focus. The man addresses the crowd and this time I focus on what he is saying.

"So, it's all in the wrist. One false move and you can cause a lot more damage than you intend to. So be careful and practice on something other than your willing partner," the man explains.

Whispered conversations erupt all around us, while people begin making their way out of the room.

Haley grabs my elbow attempting to pull me with her. Before I follow, I glance back for one last peek at the beautiful man.

Our eyes lock and we stare at each other for what feels like hours but are mere seconds.

Haley tugs my arm a little harder snapping me out of my trance.

Dropping my gaze to the floor I follow her out.

CHAPTER 3

*B*ack in the narrow hallway she leads us further down to another room. This room is quite dark, and the lighting is more like a nightclub atmosphere. She guides me to the far side of the room where we stand with our backs to the wall.

"Feel free to look around. You did so well back there. I'm going to let you speak, but please do it quietly. I don't want anyone to overhear us. Okay?"

"Sure," I whisper.

"What did you think?" she practically whispers.

"I don't know. Why didn't you warn me?" I snap.

"Would you have come if I had told you?" Haley smirks.

"Good point. But, I don't understand. Why would you bring me here?"

"You said you wanted excitement, adventure and you wanted to feel alive again. I thought this would provide all of that. Listen, don't think tonight, just take it all in. You don't have to do anything except be here. Okay?"

I feel my face heating up. "Okay."

Slowly, I take in my surroundings and the various people here. Some are dressed in business attire, a couple in various leather creations, while others are nearly naked, and some are *naked*. I wonder where the distinctions lay. *Why everyone is so different?*

Sadly, my questions will have to wait until later because I'm not supposed to be thinking and I'm going to make a consorted effort not to.

Instead, I concentrate on my facial expressions and with much difficulty I manage to remain neutral—for Haley's sake. It's difficult to do under the circumstances but somehow, I cope. Even as everyone around us appears very intimate.

I feel like a voyeur peeking in to someone's bedroom. The internal struggle to withhold my embarrassment takes all my effort, so when a man walks up to us and addresses Haley, I keep my focus on the room around me, trying in vain not to look directly at him.

"Miss Rose, it's been a while. How are you?" the gentleman asks.

"Excellent, Mr. Parker. And yourself? How have you been?" Haley responds.

"Good. Everything's been good. We've missed you at the country club."

I feel the man's gaze on me but refuse to acknowledge him. I drop my gaze to the floor because I have no idea what the protocol is for this type of situation.

"I've been quite busy lately, but I'm sure I'll be around

soon." Haley offers her standard answer for people she has no interest in—courteous but vague.

"We'll here's to soon. Take care of yourself."

I still feel the man's gaze on me until he finally walks away.

"Creep," Haley mutters under her breath.

My sentiments exactly.

She grabs my elbow and hauls me from the room. In the hallway, she drops my arm.

"Follow me. Same rules apply." Her voice returns to the cold, curt tone she's used all night.

Not only do I notice her change in tone, but her body shifts, too. It's almost as if she snaps to attention, she stiffens, and she gets a bit taller. These actions make the growing list of questions in my head.

I follow silently as she leads us down the hall and through another open door. I'm beginning to wonder if this place is made up of nothing but private rooms as we step inside and move along the back wall.

"You may look up," she offers again.

I raise my head taking in my surroundings almost fearful of what's in store. There are fewer people in this room providing me a better view.

At the front of the room is a table with a blond man perched on top of it. He's a good-looking man with a nice body. Not a body builder but someone who takes care of himself. The man is facing sideways on his knees with his hands tied behind his back. There's something in his mouth that has straps leading to the back of his head preventing him from making any sound and he's completely naked.

Another man, tall in stature with brown hair, stands beside the table with an intimidating stance as he organizes his things.

I'm curious what will be done to this man and the wait is not long.

The brown-haired man pulls a vibrator off the table of instruments, turns to his subject and begins running it up and down his bare chest.

My face begins to heat up as I struggle to keep my composure.

He concentrates on the man's nipples for a few minutes before moving it over his shoulder and down his back to the crack of his ass.

He runs the vibrator back and forth between the man's ass cheeks a few times before inserting it into him.

The kneeling man makes no sound, but I notice his eyes close tight for a moment as he takes a deep breath. Once the toy is all the way inside he appears to relax, but only for a moment before his tormentor pulls a remote out of his pocket and pushes a button.

The kneeling man flinches ever so slightly as he takes another deep breath and relaxes back into his pose.

The tormentor picks up a stick that has a fountain of strings dangling from it at one end, attached to the ends of the strings are what appear to be beads.

I fight to keep the confusion out of my expression but it's becoming more difficult.

The tormentor begins to hit the man with the apparatus

and I flinch after each snap. The tormentor moves mercilessly around his subject striking his back, ass, chest and even his penis.

The entire time the assault is taking place the man on the table doesn't move or make any sound, a fact that astonishes me.

During the demonstration, I feel someone staring at me. I fight hard not to peek but in the end curiosity wins.

In the far corner of the room, there's an odd-looking man. A man who would stand out in any room by his appearance. He has long jet-black hair that settles just past his shoulder and the palest skin I've ever seen that gives him a ghostly skin tone. He's below average in height, standing at about five foot six with a slender build—scrawny really.

There's a naked woman kneeling at his side who has a collar around her neck and it's attached to a chain. The chain leads to his left hand essentially locking her to him like a dog.

As I glance his way, his gaze locks with mine and he smiles. His smile is sinister—creepy really. I know this is not a man I want noticing me and let my gaze fall back to the ground.

I still feel his gaze on me and have a strong desire to leave. I don't think I've ever been this uncomfortable in someone else's presence before.

Before I have the chance to say the word 'Brown' to Haley, I hear a commotion coming from the direction of the strange man.

Peeking back over I see Leroy—the man who greeted us

at the door—speaking to the man and by the expression on Leroy's face he's not pleased.

After they exchange words—which are impossible to overhear—Leroy escorts the couple from the room. When they head in our direction the man glares at me with his eyebrows furrowed and forehead scrunched as if he's examining me.

With each step he takes his glare deepens until he is directly in front of me. A smile spreads across his face and he nods in my direction.

I go rigid, afraid to move or encourage the man in anyway. Relief washes through me as I observe them disappear through the door.

It takes a moment to get my bearings back and I return my attention to the front of the room. I let out a breath I didn't realize I was holding as I glance at the crowd hoping and praying no one noticed our small exchange. Just when I think our exchange has gone undetected I feel pressure on my elbow as Haley grabs me and drags me out of the room.

Apparently, she noticed.

CHAPTER 4

She hits the hallway with a stride that has me struggling to keep up. Abruptly, she comes to a halt in front of another door, pushes it open with one arm and motions me inside with the other.

I immediately recognize it's a bathroom as Haley turns and locks the door.

"What the hell was that?" she practically screams, spinning around to face me.

I'm dumbfounded and unsure how to answer.

"Alexandria, what was that?" She takes a step closer and for the first time in our friendship I'm afraid of her. This is angry Haley and I make a point never to be on the receiving end of angry Haley.

"Answer me," she snaps.

"What?" I hiss.

"Lexi that guy—what did you do?"

"Nothing. I swear, Haley. I didn't do anything,"

"What was all that about? I saw the way he looked at you," she accuses.

"I have no idea. One minute I'm watching the show, the next he's staring at me. When I looked over at him he smiled. It was so unnerving that I was about to say *'brown'* to you when Leroy approached and took him out." My feeble attempt to explain didn't even make sense to me.

"Well, that was weird." She pauses, lost in thought. "Nothing like this has ever happened before. I'm not sure what to do." She begins to pace back and forth in the small space.

"Why don't we just get out of here?" My voice shakes giving away my nervousness.

"It's not that simple, Lexi. You brought attention to yourself." Her voice is stunned, full of anxiety, which is not helping my situation.

"So?"

"So? —so, she says." She throws up her arms. "Because you're not supposed to be here," she snaps.

It suddenly dawns on me. The *rules*, the *dress apparel*, her *behavior*—everything about this night rushes to my brain. We're in trouble—big trouble.

Panic settles over me and I start to hyperventilate as I try to catch my breath. My chest becomes heavy making breathing difficult.

I walk to a bench at the side of the room and sit down taking deep deliberate breaths.

"Okay. So, what do we do?" I ask, calmly, unsure where the calmness is coming from.

"We have to go back out there. Walk to the exit and try

not to bring any more attention to ourselves." Her voice gets higher as panic takes hold. "Can you do that?"

Can I do it? Can I?

I put my hand to my chest and feel a sharp pain inside. I wonder if I'm having a heart attack as I take another deep breath.

Just as quickly as panic sets in, realty takes back over.

Wait—hold up a minute. This is just stupid. We are in a club, for God's sake. We can just walk out of here. I'm sure Haley is just overreacting. That's how rich people are —*everything* is a big deal to them.

"Okay. Let's do this," I reply, with a sudden burst of confidence. "Let's get out of here."

"All right. Remember, keep your head down," she reminds me.

"Yeah, yeah, I've got it. Let's go."

I wave her in the direction of the door.

Haley pulls the door open and steps into the hallway with me on her heels. She leads us back to the exit but as we round the corner to the common room we first arrived in—the one where the music was playing—Leroy steps into our path blocking the way.

My heart drops to my stomach as everything around us comes to a halt.

Holy shit!

CHAPTER 5

*A*s Leroy looks us over I notice Haley shudder slightly. I drop my gaze to the floor far too afraid to look at him.

I feel him scrutinizing us for a few seconds—the longest seconds of my life.

"Miss Rose, Mr. Miller would like a few words with you before you leave." His tone is firm, not exactly angry but not the friendly tone he used on our arrival either.

"Certainly," Haley answers, in an unsure voice.

They begin walking leaving me to do the only thing I can—follow them.

Nothing else is said but the tension rolling off them both is thick. That isn't helping my anxiety levels. My chest clenches, my breathing becomes heavier and my palms begin to sweat.

As we reach the end of the hall Leroy swipes his card through the slot and we stand waiting for the elevator.

Once the elevator doors open, Leroy waves us through. He steps in and the doors close behind him. He pushes the button marked 'L' and we are off.

The silence in the small space is deafening. The tension —heavy.

The doors finally open to reveal a reception area.

"Miss Rose, come with me. Miss Shaw have a seat," he says in a crass voice, pointing to a sofa that is along the side of the wall to the left.

My head snaps up at the mention of my name.

How does he know my name?

I wander over and take a seat.

Across the room Leroy pushes a door open directing Haley with a wave of his hand to enter. When she disappears, he pulls the door closed essentially shutting her inside.

He turns and gazes at me for a moment before making his way back to the elevator. I watch as he slides his card through the slot, the doors open, and he steps inside, spinning around he gives me one last look before pressing a button. The doors slide close.

I exhale deeply.

My attention returns to the door that Haley was ushered through and my mind works overtime trying to figure out what is going on in there. My heart pounds in my ears as little beads of sweat cover my forehead. I've never felt this terrified in my entire life. I have no idea what to do as I sit quietly staring at the door that is holding my best friend prisoner and will it to open.

Nothing. I can think of absolutely nothing. My mind has gone blank. My only thoughts are of what is happening on the other side of that door. My gaze remains fixed on the door and the longer I sit here the more worried I become.

I wonder if I should call someone, which only leads to more panic when I realize I don't have my phone with me. It's in Haley's car along with my purse. I have nothing. I left everything in the car. My anxiety grows as comprehension grips me leaving me shaking from head to toe. The ache in my chest returns.

Time passes slowly—although I have no way of measuring the actual time—it may have been just a few minutes, but it feels much longer. My body trembles, my heart continues to pound, my stomach is flip-flopping, and my forehead feels as if it is going to drown me in my own sweat.

Abruptly, the door opens and Haley ambles out. The expression on her face is one I've never seen before—she looks terrified, which is not helping my current state.

"Lexi. Mr. Miller would like to speak with you."

Unexpectedly, her face flashes another expression I've never seen before—helplessness. I sit staring at her for a moment wondering what I should do. *Should I make a run for it? Or should I go and see what the man wants?* My mind twists with so many thoughts that keeping them straight is impossible.

A rash decision has me determined to face this man and I begin to stand on wobbly legs. I move toward Haley and feel my face flame. I reach the door and Haley steps aside allowing me to enter.

When I'm over the threshold, Haley pulls the door closed tight, effectively leaving me alone with a total stranger.

CHAPTER 6

*I*nstinctively, I keep my gaze on the floor and remain motionless waiting for something to happen.

A rather pleasant-sounding voice with the essence of authority fills the space.

"Take a seat, Miss Shaw."

He called me Miss, but I'm too afraid to correct him, instead my head snaps up at the beautiful sound of his voice providing me a full view of the small intimate office we are in.

Mr. Miller sits across the small space, on a black leather chair, behind a large mahogany desk which is facing me. His head is down as he studies papers that sit on top of his desk.

The wall to my right has a row of mahogany file cabinets across it. The wall to my left has a large, framed, black & white photo of a woman kneeling with her back to the camera, hands behind her back and head bowed. It's a beautiful composition.

Spotting a chair in front of his desk I walk to it and take a seat. I peek across the large desk separating me from this stranger and realize the beautiful man with the piercing green eyes who caught my attention earlier is sitting across from me. I'm about to hit my breaking point and know things can't get any worse.

My heart stops beating as I stare at him. His face is stone. He doesn't look angry, but he doesn't look pleased either. He gives no indication of what is about to happen or why I'm here. Again, my mind races and I wonder what he could possibly want from me. It's not as if he knows me, although he knows my name.

I continue to scrutinize him as he looks over the paperwork on his desk.

He remains quiet, reserved, but by far the best-looking man I've ever seen and in the light of his office he is even more beautiful, if that's even possible. His eyebrows are furrowed together as he flips through several pages in the folder.

I sit wracking my brain trying to figure out what is keeping him so enthralled.

Hastily, he closes the folder placing one hand on top of it as he lifts his head up and stares directly into my eyes.

I sit stagnant, afraid to move a muscle as he continues to study me. It's a struggle to maintain eye contact but I manage—just barely.

After what seems like hours, his musical voice sounds again.

"Did you enjoy yourself, Miss Shaw?" He glares at me, while waiting.

Waiting for what? Am I supposed to answer him? I'm not sure. I have no idea what to say or do. Haley gave me no instructions for a situation such as this. The fact is, I don't think I could speak even if I wanted to. My mouth is suddenly the Sahara Desert and my mind stopped working the minute I entered the room.

He continues to examine me, not moving a muscle and I'm certain he doesn't even blink as he awaits my answer.

"Do you not speak when people ask you a question?" he asks, his voice revealing a hint of irritation.

I freeze, my gaze fixed on his and now I'm certain a blink doesn't escape me. After a moment, his expression softens a tad giving me the courage to speak.

"I'm not sure." It's the first thing that comes to my mind.

"You're not sure if you enjoyed yourself? Or you're not sure you answer people who ask questions?" Anger now crosses his features.

This is the first time in my entire life that my body and mind have completely shut down. I'm frozen to the chair. I want to answer him, to make it clear I'm not some brainless woman he can push around or scare easily. But, as I remain here, gauging him, no words come to mind. For some strange reason my body refuses to listen to my mind which is screaming to get up and get out of here.

Mr. Miller stands, armed with the mystery folder in his hand, strolls around the front of the desk and stands in front of me. He leans back to sit part way on the desk as his glare intensifies.

I've never been this tense in my life. Still frozen solid, I glare back at him unable to look away from him.

He leans over me and speaks again.

"Alexandria Lacy Shaw. Born July 19, 1986 to proud parents Renee and Harry Waters. Harry Waters a resident of Olympia, Washington and former Chief of Police in Olympia. Divorced. Mother remarried a football player named Phillip Jones. You attended Olympia high school where you graduated with honors. You next went to Cambridge University where you also graduated with honors. Married David Shaw attorney at law who has worked at Hill, Steinman and Gates for the past four years fresh out of University. You volunteer at many charities and have no children," he says all of this without ever taking his gaze off mine. I'm astounded he could remember all that information so quickly.

Once he finishes he continues to stare.

I'm left uncertain of where he is going with all these details. Hesitant if I should say anything or remain quiet. *Is he expecting me to say something?* I sit astonished that this stranger knows so much about me and I know nothing about him.

Who is this guy?

"That is just the tip of the iceberg. I know plenty more about you," he adds, with a smirk on his face as if he can read my mind. At least I think it's a smirk, in my state of mind I'm not positive of anything anymore.

Again, he stands staring at me—waiting. *What is he waiting for? An answer?* He hasn't even asked a question yet. *And, what does he mean he knows more about me?*

My mind works overtime, my face about to explode from the heat that's gathering there, and my composure is beginning to tumble fast. He stands staring at me for a few more moments and I'm about to crumble to the floor.

Then he does the unthinkable, he reaches over takes a strand of hair off my face and places it behind my ear. In that moment, as his skin touches mine, every nerve ending in my body comes alive. A jolt of electricity shoots through me making me shudder. His hand snaps back like he's been burnt, and he begins flipping through the folder again, calmly.

What the hell was that?

"What am I going to do with you now?" he asks in a softer tone and my anxiety returns in full force. The glare he gives me tells me he is waiting for an answer.

"I don't know." My voice shakes as I speak.

"You don't seem to know much, do you?" He looks at me puzzled for a moment.

He lets out a heavy sigh, stands to his full height, walks back around his desk and resumes his seat once again. He examines my face and his features twist with what seem like concern, but since he's a stranger I'm not certain.

Suddenly, he flashes a smile—a million-dollar smile—which really scares me.

"Here's what I'm going to do—" he pauses for a moment. "You're going to leave here and think about everything you saw tonight. Think hard, Alexandria. That's an order." His tone is strong, domineering, and I know I will never defy this man.

"I will give you special clearance for a couple of weeks.

If you'd like to come back, ask for Leroy at the door and he will take care of you. But—" He pauses again, gets up and wanders over to the filing cabinet, pulls open a drawer and searches for something. After retrieving a folder, he sits back down. "—I offer you a warning— this lifestyle's not for everyone. I'm a good judge of character and I can tell this is probably not something for you." His gaze burns into mine again.

"Take these with you. Read them over and think about everything you saw here tonight. These papers will give you an idea of what this world is about."

Once more, he stands from his desk, strolls around the front of it and holds the folder out to me.

I snatch it from him and flip through the documents nestled inside. It's not as if I can read one word because my mind can't focus, and my hands are shaking.

Mr. Miller wanders behind me, out of my line of vision, but I feel his gaze on the back of my head. Surprisingly the atmosphere in the room changes and in response my eyelids close. I feel him lean into me, his breath on my ear.

Fire shoots through me, as he whispers.

"This is not a place for innocence, Alexandria. And you are innocent. You should stay away from me and this place." His voice is like a symphony, his breath hitches as he moves the hair from my neck replacing it with his lips and plants a small, tender kiss there.

My eyes remain closed and I nearly melt into the chair. My insides are so tight they feel as if they are going to come bursting out but still, I remain frozen in place.

"Run from here and never look back," he whispers softly.

I feel a cool breeze across my back caused by the removal of heat from his body. My eyes spring open and catch him making his way around to his side of the desk. He sits down calmly and begins rearranging some papers. The atmosphere in the room changes back to normal and I'm left feeling more terrified than I've been all night.

"You are dismissed," he says abruptly, without any further eye contact and motions his hand at the door.

I jump out of my seat, thanking God my legs still work as I bolt for the door. I fling it open, hurry through it and close it behind me. I lean against the wood, place both hands on my knees while attempting to hang onto the folder at the same time. I drop my head down and take deep breathes trying to calm myself.

What the hell was that?

CHAPTER 7

*H*aley approaches and brushes the hair out my face.

"Are you okay, Lexi?" she asks, concern laced in her tone.

"Let's just get out of here, please."

"Sure, come on."

She immediately turns and leads me to the elevator. Once in the elevator Haley pushes a button and the doors shut.

At last, we are alone.

"What the hell happened?" she asks.

"Not here."

I'm struck by the overwhelming feeling of being watched. I glance around the elevator but can't see anything.

Arriving at our floor we step out, through the small room and into the lobby where this evening began.

Leroy is waiting for us with a smile on his face, but something tells me his smile is forced.

"Ladies. I hope you had a wonderful time," he exclaims.

"Yes, thank you, Leroy." Haley hands over the card he gave her.

"My pleasure. Please, come back soon." He reaches for her hand and shakes it.

"I will," Haley replies.

"And, Alexandria." I hold my hand out to him since he addressed me. He picks up my waiting hand, turns it over and kisses the back of it. "I hope I see you again, soon," he says with a little too much enthusiasm puzzling me.

I give him a weak smile, then turn to Haley who seems to have graced me with another look I have never seen from her before—shock.

Leroy walks ahead of us, opens the door and leads the way out.

"Bye, for now," he says, as he holds the door open.

As I walk past he winks at me.

Once outside, my body calms down rapidly. We're safe and we're out of there. I haven't been that tense, for that long, ever before and my whole-body aches. Relief washes over me when I spot the car waiting for us.

I hurry to the passenger side and fold myself in the seat. I lay the folder on my lap, pick up my purse and place it on top of the folder hoping to hide it. Haley hasn't asked about it and I'm hoping she doesn't.

Haley jumps in driver's seat and speeds away. Without a word, she drives for several miles while I stare at my hands.

Finally, she breaks the silence.

"Holy shit." Is all she says.

"You can say that again," I reply.

"Holy. Mother. Fucking. Shit," she repeats, as she whips her head back and begins laughing.

I'm stunned, as anger comes to a boiling point inside me. *How dare she laugh?* This is far from funny. *Does she not realize what just happened? Does she not realize how scared I am?* Before I know it, all emotions from the evening come spill out around me and I begin to sob.

Haley's head jerks in my direction, her gaze intense. She pulls the car over to the side of the road coming to a complete stop before ripping off her seat belt. She leans over and wraps her arms around me, hugging me tight.

"Jesus, Lexi. I'm so sorry," she exclaims.

She begins to rub my back up and down to comfort me.

"Are you, all right?" she asks.

I remain silent. My feels are a mess and I'm so confused.

"Talk to me, Lexi. Please."

I pull back from her attempting to halt the tears falling from my eyes.

"I've never been so scared in my life," I whisper.

"Me neither."

Her gaze is everywhere except on me. She hands me a tissue and I wipe my eyes and nose trying to compose myself.

"What was all that about? Who was that man?" I ask.

Her head snaps up as she gives me an odd look.

"Didn't you recognize him?" she asks, in a stunned voice.

"No, should I have?"

"That was Landon Miller—" She looks at me puzzled.

I mull that over for a moment.

"He owns Miller holdings." She rolls her eyes at me as if this is information I should know.

I run the name through my mind Miller, Miller, Miller, but still come up empty.

"Landon Miller is one of Seattle's most eligible bachelors and owner of a multi-million-dollar company—Miller holdings."

Holy shit!

I take this new information in, allowing it to digest before saying anything else.

"Well—I'm glad I didn't know that earlier," I say, with a half-smile.

"No shit," Haley laughs, again. "What did he say to you?" Her laughter ceases as she turns serious.

"I'm not sure," I answer truthfully.

"What do you mean? What did he say?"

"A lot." I pause for a moment to remember. "He knew a lot about me."

"Well, yeah. That's part of the background check," she says, dismissively with a wave of her hand.

"Background check?"

"Well, of course, Lexi. Did you really think they let just anyone in there?" she says, as if this is more information I should just know, which reignites my anger.

"Well, I don't know, Haley. If you'd given me some

information beforehand, perhaps I'd have a clue," I snap at her.

"I'm sorry. You're right. I shouldn't have done that to you." She lowers her head.

"It's okay. I can see why you did. Now answer me a question, Miss Rose. What the hell are you doing in a place like that, anyway?" I ask, raising my eyebrow.

"Oh, Lexi, that's been the one secret I've kept from you. I've been living this lifestyle for a few years now. I didn't tell you because I didn't think you would understand." She lowers her head even more.

"Haley. You're my best friend. It's not my place to understand. It's my place to accept. And I would've accepted this, if it makes you happy."

"Thank you, Lexi." She finally glances at me and smiles.

"So. What did he say to you?" I ask.

"He gave me shit for bringing you there under false pretenses. He reminded me how important anonymity is in an establishment such as that. Then he revoked my privileges for a month." Another dismissive wave of her hand.

The last statement surprises me. He took away her *privileges* but invited me back. *Why would he do that?* There is no understanding that man.

"What did he say to you?" she asks.

"He said something about this lifestyle not being for everyone, especially not the innocent ones and that I'm an innocent one. He told me to run from this place and never look back," I giggle, thinking about the absurdity of it all.

Haley giggles too and the tension in the air dissolves.

Yes, I left out a few details but there really is no harm in doing so.

Haley puts her seatbelt back on and eases the car back onto the street and heads in the direction of my house.

The closer we get to my house, the more relaxed I get.

"So, which are you?" I ask, staring straight ahead almost afraid of her answer.

"What do you mean?" she replies, her gaze shifts to mine, then back to the road.

"Do you get hit, or do you do the hitting?" I whisper.

I can't image Haley being hit by anyone, for any reason.

"It's not like that, Lexi. That's just one aspect to this life-style. There's so much more to it. It's not easy to explain." Her gaze shifts to mine once more judging my reaction. "But, just for the record," she smirks at me, as she glances back at the road, "I'm the hitter as you so eloquently put it."

I laugh—out loud. It's a reflex reaction I'm unable to stop because that is so like Haley, even though I know this is probably not a laughing matter.

CHAPTER 8

his has been the longest week of my life. After being dropped off Friday night I couldn't stop obsessing about every little thing that happened at the club. All the different types of people and the lifestyle my best friend has chosen.

The same questions are on repeat in my mind. *How did I not know of her lifestyle? Why didn't she tell me? Am I a prude? Did she really believe I wouldn't accept her anymore?* I'm astonished, overwhelmed and can think of nothing else.

But worse than all of that are the thoughts of a certain man, who if I'm being completely honest with myself, scares the living daylights out of me. As hard as I have tried to put him out of mind he floats right back at every turn. It started Friday night with non-stop dreams of him, leading to my week of analyzing every word he said to me and ending with me scrutinizing every move he made. My mind is completely consumed by him.

. . .

THERE ARE plenty of things I am certain of:

1. Landon is the best-looking man I've ever met.
2. He is telling me to stay away and never think about him or his club again.
3. He is daring me to return.

THE MAN IS a walking contradiction but what scares me the most is that he knows exactly what he's doing as he weaves his web around me.

I need to know more about the elusive Mr. Miller, so I begin with a little research on my old friend the Internet. Plugging his name into the search engine produces a lot of information, most of it pertaining to his businesses— nothing of a personal nature. There are plenty of photos of him appearing at business functions but again nothing personal. The one thing that stands out is that he's never with a woman. He always appears at functions alone.

For a fleeting second, I entertain the notion that he may be gay but quickly dismiss that idea when I think about the kiss he planted on my neck. There is no way that man is gay, he's sex personified and it drips from every single pore. There's no doubt in my mind about that.

With no personal information to go on I do the only thing left in my arsenal—I hire a private investigator. Okay, it's just a favor that a friend owes, and he happens to be an investigator. I asked him to find out any details he could on the private life of Landon Miller. It's probably over the top and I could probably be charged with stalking, but I need to know. I need to get him out of my head.

I've read over the paper-work Landon gave m, but that didn't reveal much either. There's an explanation of the lifestyle and how it works. It's odd to read how open these people talk about master's and slaves. Honestly, I thought we had banned those words from our vocabulary a hundred years ago—how truly naïve I am. BDSM is a world I have never given much consideration to and now I find myself reading and researching more. *How did that happen?* Two words—Landon Miller.

I did have one piece of personal information at my fingertips, but it just confused me more. When he gave me the package of papers about the lifestyle he included a list with the headings Hard Limits and Soft Limits.

At first it seemed like an example, but upon further examination I realize that it belongs to Landon. I don't know how I know, but there are things on the list that are consistent with the man who stood before me on Friday night.

His list surprises me. There are a lot of hard limits. Most should be obvious, breath play, fire play, things of that nature and it makes me wonder what type of person enjoys that. But, who am I to judge? To each their own I suppose. It's the small things that intrigue me most, things such as, no role switching, and no sharing are hard limits for him. Through my research I found out a hard limit is something that will never happen, and a soft limit is something that may be revisited when more trust is earned.

Armed with this small amount of information I realize two things about Landon Miller:

1) He is a one-submissive man

2) He has control issues.

After considering the lifestyle over the past week I've concluded that my life wouldn't change much if I were living this lifestyle, sad as that may be.

My husband has always wanted me home. I have no friends to speak of, except Haley. My family is non-existent. My life for the past five years has revolved around my husband and his career. I cook for him, clean for him, do his laundry, pretty much take care of every detail of his life outside of work.

Even most of my charity work helps further his career. Don't get me wrong, I love helping others but given the choice I probably would have picked different charities. The only difference between myself and a submissive is that I don't call David, Master or Sir. *How sad has my life truly become?*

On Thursday afternoon, my friend the investigator got back to me about Mr. Miller. Unfortunately, what he discovered only intensified my interest. His mother Emily is an interior designer. His father Carter is a doctor of some sorts and they've been married forever. He has two siblings Logan, who works for Miller holdings and Abbey, who is in school. That's all the information my friend could obtain about Landon Miller. The man is a mystery— a mystery that keeps me up at night.

I want to suppress these thoughts. I want to push them so far out of my mind I never think of him again. Still, I can't, which is why I'm standing in front of my full-length mirror on the next Friday night staring at myself as I ponder my reasons for going back there when everything in me is screaming for me to stay away.

I decide to be myself and dress in a regular outfit I would wear on any other night, no miniskirts or stilettos for me. Giving myself the once over in the mirror it occurs to me how wrong this is, but I don't care. It's something I need to do, and nothing will keep me away from that club tonight. I stop the battle going on inside my head and prepare myself to face the night ahead.

My husband is working late again leaving me the opportunity to leave without him asking questions.

As I leave my bedroom, I waltz down the hall to the front door, passing the side table I grab my purse and keys. I hear a horn sound coming from the driveway and make my way out the door, locking it behind me. Taking a deep breath, I saunter to the waiting cab and hop in the back seat.

After giving the address to the driver I place my head back against the seat and take another big breath. My body is already starting to tremble which fortifies my decision to take a cab rather than drive.

As we drive through town I close my eyes and wonder —not for the first time—if I'm doing the right thing. I mean for God's sakes I'm a married woman. Panic grips me as these thoughts come to mind. Is going out to obsess over a man, who is not my husband, crazy?

What the hell am I thinking?

CHAPTER 9

*J*ust as my mind is screaming *'tell the cab driver to turn around'*, I notice we've arrived. The cab crawls down the alley coming to a standstill.

The doorman appears at my door, pulls it open and offers his hand just as I pay the driver.

Stepping out of the vehicle and I'm immediately greeted by the doorman as he shuts the door.

"Good evening, Miss Shaw."

His use of my name startles me, but I do notice just like Landon last time, the doorman gets the salutation wrong, but once again, I don't bother to correct him.

"Good evening," is the only response I can muster, while I follow him to the club door.

He pulls the door open and holds it wide for me to enter.

"Leroy will be with you shortly," he declares.

"Thank you," I whisper, walking past him into the club.

The room looks the same but feels very different. There

are no *rules* to follow, no one hovering over my every move. I'm almost relaxed, until the other door swings open and Leroy steps through. He glides across the room stretching his hand out as he reaches me.

"Good evening, Miss Shaw. It's nice to see you again." Taking my hand in his, he flips it over planting a gentle kiss on the back of it, then let's go.

"Good evening, Leroy."

"Let's get you in there shall we?" he smiles.

"Okay," I answer, after being rendered speechless.

Leroy heads to what I know is an elevator to the club and I follow along.

What seemed so mysterious on my first visit now looks and feels familiar. I no longer feel scared or naïve. It's freeing this time around, almost as if I belong here.

Once in the elevator, he pushes a button and we are on our way. Uncertainty threatens to consume me, but excitement overshadows that feeling this time, until the doors open, and I notice that we're not on the same floor.

My heart pounds loudly in my chest and I wonder if Leroy can hear it given the enclosed space we are in. I try to smile at him but certain it comes out all wrong.

All kinds of thoughts run through my mind rapidly. Here I am, a woman alone with total strangers doing God knows what with God knows who. *What was I thinking coming here alone?* Nobody even knows I'm here. *What if I disappear? What if they do something to me?* Every fear pours into my mind all at once and I can feel myself pale as the blood leaves my face and my body trembles.

If Leroy notices my apprehension he doesn't show it as

he exits the elevator. Slowly, he turns around when he real-izes I'm not following. He glances up at me and smiles, a genuine smile that puts me at ease. It's irrational, I know, but I trust him. His entire aura conveys a big brother vibe that makes me feel protected. Irrational, as I've said.

"Come, Miss Shaw. This way." He motions for me to follow and against my better judgment I do.

CHAPTER 10

My legs feel like heavy boulders as my body shakes slightly and my thoughts run through my mother's stern warnings as a child. Don't talk to strangers, don't trust anyone you don't know and most importantly, don't go anywhere with someone you don't know. I'm about to break every rule she ever instilled in me.

On wobbly legs I proceed to follow him out of the elevator and I'm ever thankful I wore flats instead of the stiletto's I had to endure last time under Haley's direction.

Leroy leads the way down a long corridor through a doorway and into a large room. It's elegant, classy and not at all what you would expect in an establishment such as this.

The walls are blue and cream, subtle and calming. There are several cream-colored couches with coffee tables placed in front of them and arm chairs on either side surrounding the perimeter of the room. Tables with blue-colored table clothes and cream-colored wooden chairs are spread throughout the center of the space. In the center of every table is a glass bowl with a candle burning in it giving the entire room a warm glow. If I didn't know any better, I would think we were in an upscale bar in the center of town.

Leroy strides through the room with me dutifully following behind. There are people talking amongst themselves throughout the space, appropriately dressed this time—no leather or nakedness. My nerves resolve, and my stomach stops flip-flopping.

Leroy leads me to a bar on the opposite side of the room motioning for me to sit on the first available stool.

The bar itself, which spans the entire length of the wall, is hand carved wood and nothing short of beautiful craftsmanship. Along the bottom half are figures of people in different positions, all submissive. The top portion shines brilliantly not a nick or mark on it. Behind the bar, along the wall, are glass shelves holding different types of glasses and bottles of alcohol.

Leroy leans over the bar engaging the bartender in a short conversation. Throughout the room music plays softly in the background concealing what is being said but I manage to hear the last part.

"...very special guest." Leroy glances back at me. "You stay here until I come for you, okay?" he declares, more than asks.

"Okay," I reply, puzzled.

Leroy walks away, and I stare at his disappearing form. *What the hell was that? Very special guest? Of who?* I don't understand. It couldn't be Haley her privileges have been revoked for a month. *So, who?*

As I looked around the room deliberating the answer, it hits me like a ton of bricks—it's him. I begin searching the open space attempting to locate him, but sadly I come up short. He's nowhere to be seen. My heart clenches in my chest as I hear the bartender speaking to me.

"Here you are, Miss Shaw." He places a coaster down then a drink and gives me a wink before smiling.

"Thank you," I manage to respond, then take a sip and consider his actions.

My face scrunches up as my expression must register my shock.

"Is something wrong?" the bartender asks.

"How did—" I pause, gazing at him for a moment as I collect my thoughts. "How do you know what I drink?"

"If I tell you, I'd have to kill you." He winks, again, smiles and walks away.

Dumbfounded, I sit wondering how he knows what I drink. None of this information would be a part a background check, I'm almost positive about that. I will have to ask Haley about that at some point, after I manage to tell her about all of this.

Putting my drink and the bartender out of my mind, I search the room once more in hopes of spotting Landon. He's still not here. I'm deeply disappointed as I reach for my drink and take another sip.

A man at the other end of the bar catches my attention when he picks up his drink and makes his way over sitting down on the stool next to me. I stare at the bottle of tequila on the shelf in front of attempting to keep my gaze off the gentleman. He's staring at the side of my face making me feel uncomfortable.

"What's your name?" he asks, with a gentle tone.

"I don't think it would be wise to tell a stranger my name in a place like this," I declare, shifting my gaze to him for a second then returning my attention to the bottle.

"You're probably right." I see him bow his head in apology then quickly fixes his gaze back on me. "Forgive me, it's just that you are the most beautiful woman I've seen in a long time," he smiles.

I twist slightly on the stool to face him almost offended by his statement.

"Does that line really work?" I force an awkward smile.

"Actually, more often than it should," he laughs a little. "My name is Jason." He holds his hand out in offering.

I extend my hand to his but am abruptly pulled off my stool.

"Time to go," Leroy commands, a scary tone in his voice.

As I right myself to keep from falling over, Leroy grabs my hand locking his grip tight around mine.

"Hey. We were having a conversation," Jason practically shouts at Leroy.

"Conversation's over. Have a good evening." Leroy forces a smile.

He tugs me along leading the way out of the room. I'm frightened as I stumble along trying to keep up. His grip is strong and locked on my hand. Breaking his hold —impossible.

*a*bruptly, Leroy stops walking, drops my hand from his grasp, takes a deep breath and turns to face me.

"Sorry about that," he offers, his face relaxing.

I'm stunned by the sudden change in his demeanor and confused by how quickly his moods change.

"Should I be here?" I whisper.

Leroy simply smiles then begins walking again as he calls over his shoulder, "This way."

Even though I'm a little surprised by his response, I follow anyways knowing the answer to my question is a resounding 'no,' but I can't find it in myself to care.

We walk along several corridors that honestly have me feel like we're walking in circles. Finally, Leroy heads into a room that is the same as the one we just left, but with less people. He leads me to a bar once again, where my drink is now sitting on a coaster waiting for me. I sit on a bar stool trying to hide my astonishment.

"Why did you move me?" I ask.

"This side of the bar is better." He turns with smile on his face. "I'll be back for you in a little while. Enjoy yourself. And stay put, please." He doesn't wait for a response before he turns and walks out of the room.

I sit and wonder what he means by '*better*,' I mean, the room is identical to the other one. It makes me wonder why someone would make such a design choice.

As I glance around the room I notice less people in here but nothing else seems different. He also told me to stay put. *Did he mean on this bar stool, in this room, or the club altogether?* This is not how I planned this evening going and I'm quite confused.

As time passes, the bartender never allows my drink to be empty, filling it every time it seems to be close. Although, he never asks for payment, which I can only assume is because he's running a tab. At least I hope he is. My mother's oldest saying pops into mind.

Nothing is free, Lexi. There's always a price to pay.

Judging my life up until this point, she was so right. I have paid a price for the choices I've made, and it isn't until now, as I'm re-evaluating some of my choices, do I realize how high those prices have been. But dwelling on all of this will change nothing and my only goal is to fix everything somehow, which is what brought me here in the first place.

I'm quite certain my choices now will come at a high price, but as I sit on this bar stool praying that a certain man makes an appearance tonight, even though I have a husband at home, I don't care. If you asked me a week ago if this is where I'd be, I would have told you that you were insane—and yet, here I sit.

The music flowing through the room is soothing as is pours through the top-notch system. I watch people mingling, but talking doesn't appeal to me now, so I remain where I was told to stay.

As I glance around the room once again, I notice another man staring at me. He holds my attention for a moment before I quickly turn towards the bar and pick up my drink. I really don't want anyone to notice me. Well, only one man but he's not here.

When I put my drink down, I feel a hand on my shoulder that makes me jump and I spin my head around to see who it is.

"Sorry. I didn't intend to startle you," the man says, he's the same one who was staring at me. He's an older gentleman, probably in his forties, maybe fifties. He's wearing a very nice tailored suit and a big smile on his face.

"That's all right. I'm okay," I give him a small smile.

"I saw you from across the room and was intrigued by your beauty." He reaches for my hand, gently raising it to his lips, placing a soft kiss on it.

"Um—thank you," I say awkwardly, wondering what it is with the men in this place and their old fashion gestures. *Who kisses a woman's hand these days?*

"Are you here with anyone?" he asks, as he glances around the room.

My body tenses and I suddenly realize I don't know how to respond. *Am I here with anyone?* Technically no, but I don't want to give him the wrong impression. I most certainly don't want him to think I'm looking for anyone, either. *How do I answer him? What do I say?* In all my hours obsessing over this place in the past week this scenario never crossed my mind. It was only Landon I saw in my head, it never occurred to me that I would be here alone and appear alone.

The man must notice my internal dilemma.

"I'm sorry. I shouldn't have asked you that. It's all right if you don't answer. I'll tell you what—" He reaches into the inside the pocket of his suit, pulls out a card and hands it to me, "—this is my card. Call me if you would like to get together."

The man smiles and walks away quickly, leaving me frozen to the bar stool staring at his card. He was soft spoken, kind and not bad looking for a man of his age. I must admit this place is doing wonders for my ego.

As soon as that thought enters my mind, another quickly takes hold.

You know what he wants from you!

That quickly deflates my ego.

In a flash, the card I'm holding is ripped from my hand. I whip my head around to see who took it.

"Evening, Miss Shaw." His soft, warm, voice wraps around me like a caress.

There he stands, the man who has invaded my dreams, my life for that matter. My memory didn't do him justice, I notice as he stands very close to me, his gaze staring directly into mine.

Instantly, my heart flutters and my blood races faster through my veins spreading fire from the top of my head to the tips of my toes. I lower my gaze to my drink to compose myself, a huge mistake on my part because trembling hands are impossible to hide when trying to hold a drink.

"Evening, Mr. Miller." I manage to squeak out.

"Please. Call me, Landon," he states, as he picks up my hand, placing a gentle kiss on it.

"Lexi," is my only response, as I contemplate another man kissing my hand. I feel like we've jumped back fifty years.

"Lexi," he repeats, my name rolling off his tongue quite pleasantly. "Well, Lexi, you won't be needing this."

He tosses the business card on the bar and the bartender is quick to pick it up.

I give him an annoyed look. "Why did you do that?"

"I'm sorry. Did you want to call him?" He smirks at me like he's in on some joke I'm not privy to.

"Well, no, but—"

"Well then, I was right. You won't be needing it." And there it is, his signature smirk that makes me wonder if I'm missing something. "You know, I honestly didn't think I would see you here again," he reveals, as his gaze pierces mine, but there is something behind his eyes that I can't place.

What does he mean by that? Does he not want to see me here again?

"Neither did I."

"Did you read the literature I gave you?" His tone turns serious.

"Yes," I answer, my face flames thinking of all the things I've read and seen regarding this lifestyle.

"Since you were here last week, and you've read what I gave you, I assume your curiosity hasn't been fulfilled. Am I correct?"

Landon side steps gracefully around my stool to stand in front of me. His face inches closer from mine, close enough to feel his warm breath wash over it. My body's in shock and so tense it's almost painful, but still I'm unable to move a muscle.

"I um—I just came—" My gaze immediately falls to the ground.

I can't look at him and have no idea how to answer. The truth is I'm here to see him, but I can't tell him that—he can't know the truth. How can I explain that he is all I think about, dream about, knowing that all he wants is another submissive to train. He doesn't want the truth, least of all, my truth.

"Alexandria." My name falls from his lips like an embrace making my insides boil. He lifts my chin with his finger, raising my head to look at him. "I told you this was not the place for innocence. These men will eat you alive." And his signature smirk back in place.

His voice is gentle, caring, a complete contrast to the meaning behind his words. I'm of two minds, one being a complete mess, almost a puddle on the floor, and two angry, offended and downright pissed off. *How dare he assume anything about me?* He doesn't even know me.

"I'm not innocent. I wish you would stop saying that," I exclaim, curtly.

"Oh, but you are. Trust me, I know innocent when I see it." His annoying signature smirk turns into a smile—a condescending smile.

Landon turns and waves the bartender over. I stare at him bewildered by his rude statement. He looks back assessing my face for a moment.

"Hey, don't be offended. I think it's sweet," he says, and flashes his million-dollar smile.

My anger flares even more. Sweet—he just referred to me as sweet. Now I'm not only innocent but sweet also. I'm far from sweet and innocent. I mean really, aren't I the one who is married here? So big deal he whips people and gets off on it. *Does that make him bad? Does that make him more experienced than me?* Well, I suppose it does, in this area at least, but that still doesn't mean I'm sweet and innocent.

I peek up at Landon as he is taking a sip of his cocktail. I'm suddenly aware of how his lips form around the glass and find myself wishing I was the glass. I want his lips on me.

What the hell is wrong with me?

"Someday, Alexandria. Someday." He raises an eyebrow.

I hear his words but can't believe them. It's as if he's read my mind. No, he can't. *Can he?* That's just ridiculous.

"Someday what?" I ask, curiosity dripping from my tongue.

"Never mind." He brushes off my question as he plasters his signature smirk across his face once more. "Come, I'd like to show you around."

Landon holds out his hand to me and what bothers me the most is not that he seems to be making fun of me, not that he appears full of himself, arrogant even. No what bothers me even more than all of that is I take his hand without any hesitation, ready to follow this man wherever he wants to take me.

As soon as my hand touches his, heat rushes up my arm. I gasp as I peer up at him in shock, but he just squeezes my hand tighter, tugging me off the barstool. If he feels the heat, he isn't letting on.

CHAPTER 12

As we walk out of the room Landon let's go of my hand and places his on the small of my back leading me forward. I feel faint as the heat flows throughout my body. My entire frame is trembling slightly, and my knees are growing weaker as we walk. I wish lightening would strike me at this moment because I know Landon will notice my reaction to his touch and use it to his advantage, however that may be.

Landon leads us into the elevator, pressing a button which makes the doors close, leaving us encased in the small space. The atmosphere shifts as I peek up at him.

He stares at me with an expression on his face I can't understand. I feel all the energy in the room pulling me towards him as I struggle to remain in place.

Faster than I can comprehend, I throw myself against him and he hits the elevator wall. I hold him prisoner against the wall pressing my body into his.

He places one hand on my hip, the other on my shoulder and just when I think he's going to push me away he lunges forward his lips locking with mine in the most passionate kiss I have ever had.

In response my hands shoot around his neck as I kiss him back. He takes my bottom lip between his and I think my insides will explode from the heat we are generating. His tongue darts out moving along my lip asking for entrance. I quickly grant him permission by releasing my tongue to join his.

A soft moan escapes me as Landon grunts shifting his hips further into mine. I tangle my hands in his hair as his hands move all over my body.

I know that if something doesn't stop us soon I will completely lose my mind leaving me no choice but to throw him to the floor and rip the clothes from his body.

Landon swiftly spins us around and pulls away leaving me gasping for breath and confused. My head falls forward, my breathing is out of control and my mind is spinning. I wonder why he stopped us.

Abruptly, the doors to the elevator open and Landon steps out looking back at me while waiting. *Is he not affected at all by what just happened?* I am completely annoyed that I seem to be the only one aroused here.

I step out of the elevator on shaky legs and wait for Landon to show me where we are going next.

Instantly he takes my hand leading the way down the corridor. He stops outside of a room, placing his hand on the small of my back and leading me inside. Once inside he guides me toward the other side of the room.

We are in a demonstration room that is crowded but Landon guides us to an area with plenty of space. I glance up at him and notice his full attention is on the front of the room.

Shifting my gazes, I search for what holds his interest.

Leisurely, people are filtering their way out of the room. I peek up at Landon whose gaze remains on the front of the room. I look forward once more as the people in front of us begin parting making their way out. As the space in front of me clears I'm able to see is a table where there is a naked woman tied to it and spread-eagled. There is a man untying her right wrist and as he does he rubs it gently with cream. He moves to her left wrist and repeats the process.

I feel hot breath on my ear. Heat spreads along my backside as Landon moves directly behind me pressing his whole body against mine.

"It's aftercare. Probably, the most important part of what we do," he whispers.

I continue to watch as the man moves to the woman's right leg releasing it from it from a cuff and rubbing it in the way he did with her wrists. It is one of the most sensual scenes I have ever witnessed. The effort he takes in making certain she is cared for is clear.

"If this lifestyle is practiced properly it can be very plea-surable for both parties," Landon continues, as he presses his body tighter to mine. "If practiced badly it can be very dangerous," he warns.

Landon wraps his arms around my waist pulling me impossibly closer. I can feel his erection nudging my backside as he nibbles on my earlobe. I want nothing more than to turn around and kiss him but can't seem to take my eyes off the man and woman at the front of the room.

The man is now massaging her entire body as she remains still. My hands move unconsciously to Landon's thighs and are now rubbing up and down them. He is breathing heavily in my ear, but it is my breathing that is embarrassingly out of control.

"Looks like the show is over," he whispers.

I feel a cool breeze down my backside as Landon steps out of the embrace leaving me with a sense of loss. The connection we had is broken and I want more. No—I need more.

When I turn around to plead with him there is only empty space where he was. I quickly scan the room, but he is nowhere to be found. My brain begins to wonder if I imagined it all and have almost convinced myself that I'm losing my mind when Leroy appears in front of me.

"Mr. Miller apologizes for his quick exit, but he had some business to attend to," Leroy explains with a smile.

"Oh. Okay." The rejection heavy in my voice.

I glance around the room wondering what I should do now.

"If you would like I can return you to the bar until he is finished." Leroy offers.

"Um… sure, that would be great," I reply.

Leroy leads me from the room and we make our way back to the bar. For the third time this night I sit on a barstool and wonder what I am doing here? Having just made out with a man who is not my husband and is now waiting for him to return so we can do it again.

The bartender pours me another drink as I sit and contemplate the mess my life is quickly becoming. Guilt floods me as I think about my intimate moment with Landon. Well, it was intimate to me. *I* wonder if he feels the same. Perhaps, this is an every weekend occurrence for him, or maybe he does this stuff all the time. Why wouldn't he? I mean, he can have any woman he wants. He probably has a line waiting for him. Maybe he's with one right now. I hadn't considered that. The thought never crossed my mind.

I glance around the room and notice there are even fewer people here than before. I wonder where everyone went as I glance at my watch for the first time this evening.

"Holy shit," I practically scream out.

Hastily, I jump off the stool and start franticly looking between the door and the bar uncertain of what to do.

The bartender notices my panicked state.

"Is everything all right, Miss Shaw?" he asks.

"Uh, yes. I just have to get out of here. I didn't realize how late it was," I answer, as I grab my purse, open it and start digging around for money.

"Actually, it's rather early. Two thirty in the morning early, to be exact," he laughs.

I remain frantic as I dig further into my purse and come up with my wallet.

"How much do I owe you?" I ask.

"Oh, nothing. It's all taken care of," he smiles.

"Don't be ridiculous, you must have run a tab?" I

counter, as I peer up at him with a twenty in my hand and sarcasm dripping in my tone.

"No, there was no need to. Like I said, it's all taken care of. Would you like me to call Leroy and have him escort you out?" he offers.

"That won't be necessary," I reply, as I begin to walk away.

"Miss Shaw," the bartender calls out, as I'm half way to the door.

"Yes," I answer, turning back to face him.

"You can't get in the elevator without a card," he smirks at me.

"Oh, right. Okay, I'll wait." I make my way back to the stool and take a seat.

"Don't worry, he won't be long," he smiles, again.

"Thanks."

Although, I didn't see the bartender leave his post or use a phone to my utter astonishment Leroy arrives in short order to escort me out of the club.

"Did you have a nice evening?" he asks, as we walk.

"Yes, I did. Thank you." I smile.

As we make it to the door of the club I turn to shake Leroy's hand. He has other plans as he pulls my hand to his lips and plants a kiss on it.

"Mr. Miller, apologizes, once more, for not being available. He hopes you feel free to return anytime. He has also arranged your transportation home." Leroy smiles as he opens the door to the alley.

Already waiting outside in the alleyway is a big black limousine. Shock is an understatement. I'm stunned.

"That's not necessary, really. I can take a cab," I plead.

"Its fine, Miss Shaw. It's all taken care of," Leroy says, as he ushers me to the limo and makes certain I get inside.

"Have a good evening. I hope we see you again, soon." He closes the door before I can respond.

CHAPTER 13

I am overwhelmed, entirely out of my element. I sit and watch as the driver pulls down the alley and heads out into the city.

Wow… a limo. That man knows no bounds. I'm immediately pulled from my haze when I realize we are not heading in the direction of my house. Quickly, I scan outside my window to make certain I'm correct. Panic sweeps through me as I search for the button that brings the partition down, shielding me from the driver. After locating it I push the button and the driver comes into view.

"Excuse me. You seem to be heading the wrong way."

"Yes, Miss Shaw. I was informed of your address. If you sit back, we have a quick stop to make and then I will return you home." The driver gives smiles at me.

"Okay," I whisper, filled with uncertainty but feel I have no other choice now.

Still in a panic I sit back and watch out the window wondering where we are heading.

The driver takes us through the downtown core to the other side of the city. My knowledge of this side of the city is limited as I watch the streets pass by.

He pulls into a neighborhood that is rather charming with modest houses. It seems like a nice quiet place. He parks along the curbside in front of a house that is quite cute, a white picket fence and all.

What immediately catches my attention is the car in the driveway. The car looks oddly familiar as I stare in disbelief—it can't be.

As the door to the house opens, my husband steps on to the porch. I look on bewildered. *What is he doing here?*

Out of the door steps another person, a woman. A woman I know all too well—Laura. Laura is my husband's paralegal. David leans in and kisses her passionately.

I am stunned, devastated and angry. This does not look like something that has just happened. In fact, these two seem awfully familiar with each other like this has been going on for a long time.

I must get out of here. I can't watch any longer.

"Can you take me home, please?" I beg the driver.

He simply nods and pulls the car away from the curb. I fall back against the seat and bury my head in my hands.

CHAPTER 14

*I*n life, all things come to an end some in good ways and some bad. What happened the week following the discovery of my husband's affair fell somewhere between the two leaving me a lack of clarity.

After waking up from a restless night's sleep I realize it's good because my marriage is ending but then again, it's bad because my marriage is ending. I really can't explain how I am feeling and if I had to sum it up with just one word I would say I'm numb. I feel nothing. There's no sadness. I'm not angry. I just feel empty about my marriage ending. However, I never thought I would be on the verge of being thirty years old and looking forward to divorce.

When I saw David leaving that whore's house I was shocked. I truly believed he was incapable of doing something like that but after witnessing it with my own eyes I must admit I didn't know him after all. To make matters worse when he came home last night I felt I had no right to confront him after my own behavior the last evening.

Playing the coward, I pretended to be asleep when he came into the bedroom.

Upon waking this morning I'm fuming, and all hell is about to break loose. With no sleep and a lot of time to think I am pissed. Thoughts ran through my mind all night of all the times he didn't come home—working late, yeah right—every excuse he used. I can't believe I was so stupid. Well, no more. He had to leave once and for all. There will be no excuses and no mind games. I am done and ready to move on with my life. As for David—it wouldn't be that simple.

At first, he thought he could talk his way out of the situation.

"Lexi, it just happened. I swear to God nothing like this has ever happened before. I love you. Please…"

Blah, blah, blah—is all I hear.

David and I are standing in our living room, there are three meters between us, but we might as well be cities apart.

As I look at him I wonder why I haven't noticed certain things until now, like how small he appears. I've never had to look up at him like I do with Landon. I have no urge to grab him and hold on tight like I do with Landon. It seems odd to me that I'm willing to let go so easily until he opens his mouth and lets the lies fly out then it becomes painfully clear.

"Just give us a chance, Lexi. For Christ's sakes, we've been married for five years," he pleads.

"Five years. That's right—" I yell, "—and how many of those five years have you been cheating on me?"

"I just told…" he attempts to say before I cut him off.

"Don't bother. It doesn't matter now. I'm done. Finished." I take a deep breath, trying to calm myself. "Look David, our marriage has obviously been over for a long time. I'm not willing to drag this out any further. So please—just go." I'm exhausted from my sleepless night.

As David tentatively moves in the direction of our bedroom, I flop down on the couch. I have nothing left to say and rehashing this isn't getting us anywhere. Laying my head on the back of the couch I search the ceiling for any kind of answer. I must be completely honest with myself and admit that I just don't care anymore. As far as I'm concerned, our marriage has been over long for a long time. The only reason it hasn't ended is fear. I have become complacent living the same routine afraid to make a change which was fine for a period but I'm so over that now. Now I want a life, a real life where I can make being happy a priority.

I guess the person I must thank for my enlightenment is Haley. Thanks to her I met Landon Miller and from the moment I met him, he made me feel alive again. Every thought, every fantasy now stars Landon Miller. I can't stop thinking about him and it's driving me insane.

Ending my marriage is easier now after admitting what I've been missing, things I want in my life badly. I know, after one night at that club I can no longer live without these things. I can no longer live without Landon Miller in my life. How I intend to make that happen is uncertain, but I know come hell or high water, I will.

As I sit on the couch listening to my husband pack his

clothes my only thought is what I'll do next. I almost feel bad that my marriage is ending while my mind is on another man but after witnessing my husband's display last night guilt is now on the back burner.

In truth, I am still angry at David but I'm also a little bit relieved. I suppose in some small way this is a blessing in disguise. If we both move on, then it will make what comes next a lot easier. Getting a divorce can be a complicated process but, in our circumstance, I don't anticipate any problems.

When David finishes packing his belongings, he piles them in his car and returns to the living room. The slamming of the front door signals what I hope is our final round.

"Alexandria. I'm ready to go," he announces, and I cringe hearing him say my full name. "Are you sure this is what you want?" he questions.

I find it hard to look at him. Even though, I'm no angel in this scenario his display proves how long I've been a fool and it hurts. Being betrayed no matter how long it goes on doesn't sit well with me. I never ask for details because honestly, I don't want to know. What I witnessed last night are all the details I need. I just want him gone.

"I'm sure," I reply meekly.

"Well—I guess I'll make arrangements to get the rest of my stuff when I get settled somewhere," he says, as he crosses the room and stands in front of me.

I remove my head from the back of the couch and stand looking down at the floor. Refusing to meet his gaze.

"That's fine. Let me know when," I answer, trying to

keep my voice from wavering. 'Keep it together,' is the statement on repeat in my mind. David's a lawyer he will search for any sign of uncertainty and if I give any indication that I'm having doubts he'll use that to his benefit.

"Fine," he hisses, his tone laced with anger.

I can't fathom why he is angry. After all it's he who ruined this marriage. He is the one who played me for a fool. He is the one who has been seeing someone else for God knows how long.

I refuse to allow him to make me feel guilty over this situation. He will have to take responsibility for this one. Besides he's probably angry that I won't allow him to state his case. There's no way he can win and that would anger him more than our marriage ending.

"I'll let you know where I'm staying."

"Fine."

"Fine," he spits out with such distain as he turns to heading for the door and as it slams shut I know it's over.

Nerve that's what I would call it. He thought I would feel bad. *Dreamer.* I stand up walk to the front window and watch as he pulls his car out of the driveway.

CHAPTER 15

*J*f I had to define how I am feeling at this moment the only word that comes to mind is relieved. Relieved that this is over, relieved that it will be quick and painless and relieved that my life can begin again. I didn't realize how boxed in I truly felt until this happened but the moment he walked out the door all I feel is relieved and it feels great.

The rest of the night is spent boxing up most of David's belongings and putting them in the garage. I want a fresh start and having his stuff around only reminds me of what happened. I feel the need to cleanse myself of him.

I know we still have some things to sort out but I'm confident that we'll be able to do that amicably because once all the dust settles I believe we'll both realize how unhappy we've been.

Once I'm finished with David's stuff I make my way to the bedroom to retire for the evening. After brushing my teeth and washing my face I put my pajama's on and hop into bed.

I've never had a problem falling asleep alone because David often came home from work late. It really was stupid of me not to realize sooner what was really going on. I suppose I didn't want to know.

As my eyes close my mind drifts to the same place it has been going for the past two weeks. Landon appears in my head as I drift off to sleep thinking about the kiss we shared in the elevator last night.

CHAPTER 16

I'm jolted awake Sunday with what I'm sure is a nightmare, but I can't remember the details.

I get up from the bed and shuffle my way to the bathroom spinning the tap to turn on the water in the shower. I step out of my pajamas and into a nice hot spray. The water cascading over me feels wonderful as I stand in a dream state for quite a while.

Eventually I snap out of my daze and finish my business. Stepping out of the shower I dry myself with a towel before walking through the bedroom to the closet to pick out an outfit to wear.

After I'm done dressing I return to the bathroom to do something with my hair deciding a ponytail would do the trick since I have no plans to go anywhere.

Leaving the bedroom, I make my way to the kitchen and start a pot of coffee. Once the coffee is brewing I move on to the living room and remove the book I've been reading off the bookshelf and place it on the couch for my return.

I return to the kitchen and make myself a wonderful smelling cup of java perfect for relaxing with a book. Arriving back in the living room I plop down on the couch and place the coffee on the end table as I pick up my book and begin reading.

After reading could no longer hold my attention, I sit lounging on the couch. One day after my husband left our marital home panic sweeps through me and I wonder if I made the wrong decision. I gave him no chance. I never allowed him to explain. I simply told him to get out and not come back.

Now I am having doubts. Maybe I should have talked to him, perhaps let him have his say. Could I have been too quick to dismiss him? Did I judge him too harshly? After all, wasn't I the one thinking about another man for two weeks? Wasn't I making out with another man on the same night I saw my husband at his mistress's house?

As these thoughts float through my mind the doorbell shrieking throughout the house rescues me. Tentatively, I rise from the couch to answer the door.

Standing on my doorstep is a man holding a glorious bouquet of flowers.

"May I help you?" I ask.

"I have a delivery for Alexandria Shaw," the man says.

I stand staring at the man for a moment before reaching for the vase. Still stunned I stare at the flowers for another moment until I see the man walking away.

"Oh, please wait. I'll get you..."

The man interrupts me immediately.

"That's fine. It's all been taken care of," he says, as he waves his hand and strolls back to his delivery van.

I turn and walk back into the house closing the door with my foot.

I place the flowers on the coffee table and sit back on the couch starring at them.

There is a note attached but I'm too afraid to read it. I struggle with all the crazy thoughts running through my mind. Finally telling myself how stupid I'm being thinking they can't possibly be from Landon. *Why would he be sending me flowers?* I'm also hoping they're not some last-ditch effort David's behalf.

Reaching for the note my hand trembles as I pluck the envelope from the middle of the arrangement. I slide my finger along the seam creating an opening to pull out the small card. I instantly know who they are from by the elegant script staring back at me.

Life is never what it seems. My condolences.

What the hell does that mean? Relief washes through me as I realize they are not from David.

That only leaves one possibility.

Landon.

But, how can he know?

It seems this man knows more about my life than I do and yet he remains a complete mystery to me. *How will I figure out the puzzle that is Landon Miller?*

There is one person that may have some insight about Landon but I'm not sure I can ask her without offering too much information on my part. Information is not something I'm willing to part with currently. I guess the truth is I really don't have much information to offer. I have no idea what is going on between us.

I pick up the phone and dial Haley's number.

She answers on the second ring.

"Hey girl. Where have you been?" she asks.

"Around. Are you busy today?"

"What's wrong?" she quickly asks.

"I need you."

"I'm on my way." The line goes dead.

I sit back reading the card again then stare at the flowers some more.

CHAPTER 17

*H*alf an hour later Haley sits beside me on the couch glancing between the small card in my hand and the flowers predominately displayed on my coffee table.

"Well. Are you going to tell me who they're from and what is going on?" she finally asks, after a few minutes of silence.

"It's a long story."

"Okay. Spit it out," she urges.

"David's gone."

"Gone where?"

"He left. I told him to leave yesterday and he did." I sigh, pressing my fingers against my forehead trying to rub away the stress. "I saw him with another woman on Friday night," I explain, while lowering my head.

"What?" Haley snaps, apparently as shocked as I am.

"I was coming home Friday night and I saw him leaving

Laura's house and let's just say they weren't having a business meeting," I explain.

"What the hell?" Haley hisses.

"I know. I know. I wouldn't have believed it if I hadn't seen it."

"Well, I'm not surprised, really. I told you there was something about him. I'm just surprised I didn't see this sooner. He flew right under my radar. I hate that," she rambles on thoughtfully, for a moment.

I sit quietly thinking about what she is saying. She's right. *How could I have missed this?* I've thought about that a lot in the past two days since seeing David my thoughts always go to the same place—coming up with the same conclusion—I truly don't care. I don't care how it happened. I don't care why it happened and to be quite frank thinking about it doesn't change anything either. I'm done trying to figure out how I missed it all because it won't do any good at this point anyway. Also—if I'm being completely truthfully—my feelings where this marriage is concerned were over long ago.

"Hey, it's okay. I'm not going to dwell on this. I'm going to move forward from this." I place my hand on her knee as reassurance.

"I know. I'm still pissed off though." She scrunches her face tight in thought. "Hey, you never told me how you caught him?"

Knowing this would come up I'm still uncertain how much information to give her. There's no doubt she'll be angry I kept my trip to the club from her, but even more so, the fact I never told her about what Landon has done for me. I really don't want to tell her now, but I guess there's no way around it. There's no doubt once her ban is lifted at the club she'll be back and will see what's going on first hand.

Explaining everything first is for the best. So, with a pit in my stomach and a lump forming in my throat I begin.

"Haley. There's something I have to tell you, but you have to promise me you won't get mad," I plead.

"Okay."

"I mean it. Promise me."

"All right. I promise. Just tell me." Her voice gives away her agitation.

"The night we went to the club I wasn't exactly honest about what happened with Mr. Miller."

"What do you mean?" she asks, concern laced in her tone.

And like a dam bursting I spill. Every detail pours out about what happened with Landon and me that night, right up until this past Friday night. I tell her how I found out about David and how it led to him moving out yesterday.

When I finish, she sits silently staring at me, no expression on her face, giving me no indication to what she is thinking or feeling. It's unnerving to see her this way as I anxiously wait for her to say something. Anything.

After what seems like hours she leans forward, putting her elbows on her knees, her head in her hands, and lets out a sigh—actually more of a groan.

I sit nervously watching her reaction closely. My stomach twists in pain, my hands balled into fists so tight my nails are digging into my palms. Her reaction means everything to me. I have already lost my husband this week. To lose my best friend too—I can't handle that. Not today.

"Jesus, Lexi. Why didn't you tell me before?"

"I don't know. I guess I was scared." I'm relieved that she's still talking to me. Thankful that she hasn't gotten up and walked out the door yet.

"Scared of what?" Her voice raises a few octaves.

"Of how you would react. I'm married woman lusting after an unattainable man. What was I supposed to say?" My voice comes out a little louder than necessary.

"I get it, but it's me we're talking about. You could have told me." I can hear the disappointment in her tone.

Relief is quickly replaced by remorse. I feel horrible because she's right, I should've told her. She's never judged me before and I should've known she wouldn't now either. The truth is she probably would have encouraged it from the start. I don't know why I didn't tell her. There really is no explanation for behavior.

"I know. I'm sorry I didn't tell you. It was wrong of me. Can you forgive me?"

"Of course. But, more importantly tell me what you really think of Landon Miller?" She waggles her eyebrows as a huge smile spreads across her face.

And this is what I love most about Haley. She never holds a grudge and she understands me. At this moment all I see is my old friend who wants details on a guy I may like.

Her face has gone from confusion to excitement in a matter of seconds.

"What do you want to know?"

"Everything. Tell me everything. You must really like him if you were willing to go back there—alone?"

"Yeah, I do. Like him that is. But I don't know Haley, our time together has been short, and I know nothing about him. Somehow he seems to know an awful lot about me though." I give her a hard glare.

"Well, that could be because of the paper work I filled out on you." She has the decency to look ashamed as she shares this information.

"I would believe that to be true if it weren't for some of the small things he seems to know," I respond.

"What do you mean?" She looks at me curiously.

"Well, for example, he knows my preferred drink. He knew whenever someone talked to me—at the club I mean," I take a deep breath. "He always seems to know where I am, and he knew about David and his whore—" I trail off, unable to finish that sentence.

Her eyebrows scrunch together deep in thought. Then she her eyebrows raise almost to her hairline.

"He's watching you," she simply says.

Now it's my eyebrows to pull together.

"What?"

"It makes perfect sense. He's watching you." She shrugs.

"But—how?" I wonder.

"My dear, that whole club is covered with cameras." She shrugs again.

I suddenly feel stupid as what she says dawns on me.

"Oh, of course. But why? I mean why would he be watching me?"

"Well, duh. He likes you too." An enthusiastic smile spreads across her face.

"No. I mean, no way. I don't know him, and he doesn't know me. Why would he be interested in me when he could have anyone? For, Christ sakes, I'm married."

"Evidently he doesn't care about that. Look what he did," she says with a smirk on her face.

"He didn't do anything. David did," I answer puzzled.

"Yes, but Landon made sure you found out. Didn't he?" She's still wearing an irritating smirk.

"Oh my God, Haley. What else do you think he knows?" I ask, suddenly nervous again.

"From what I know about Landon, you can bet he knows everything there is to know about you. The man is thorough, there's no doubt about that."

"Holy shit," I think back on some of our meetings. "You have to tell me everything you know about him, Haley. Everything."

"It's not much, he's a pretty private man. The basics are he owns the club and another business, Miller Holdings. His parents are still together, and I believe they've been married for like forty years or more. He has a brother and a sister. He's a member at the country club but I rarely see him there, unless there is some sort of celebration with his family. The only place I ever see him is the club and believe me when I say even that is on rare occasions." She finishes talking and glances at me.

"What do you mean it's a rare occasion you see him at the club?"

"I mean I know he's there every weekend, but he rarely comes out of his office and he almost never mingles with club guests."

I am completely confused since going to the club for the past two weekends, he's been out in the club with me both times. As I think about it he didn't mingle with anyone else, but he escorted me to a scene. What she is saying doesn't make sense.

"Isn't he a Dom?"

"Well, yes. But I've never seen him with a permanent sub," she replies.

"What do you mean?"

"He does demonstrations at the club but not very often. He's also had girls by his side on occasion. But I've never seen a collared sub with him. Ever."

"Wow. I wonder why that is?" I mutter, speaking mostly to myself.

"There are rumors, of course." She examines her nails trying to appear uninterested but it's not working.

"What rumors?"

Her gaze never leaves her nails as she maneuvers into gossip mode.

"You know most of this is probably just gossip and let me tell you the elite love to gossip. The juicier the better but I've heard a few stories in my time at the club." Her gaze finally leaves her nails as she looks right at me. "I've never believed most of them myself because please—as if," she waves her hand dismissively. "One is that he is gay and that is why we never see a permanent sub," she laughs.

I look at her, confused. Even if he was gay, surely, he would have a sub.

"Hiding." She makes air quotes with her fingers as she says the word.

"Oh."

"Yeah I know. It's ridiculous, of course," she laughs again.

I must agree with her because there is no way Landon Miller is gay. Not that there would be anything wrong if he were, but I have it on pretty good authority this is not the case.

"I suppose the longest running gossip would be he's just a playboy who runs around with different women all the time. They say he'll never settle down. It's not in his nature. Personally, I think he just respects privacy. He gives other people privacy by providing a private club and expects privacy from those closest to him. Living the lifestyle, we do I understand the need for privacy. If what he is became public, his life would be a living hell. I understand why he is the way he is, and I respect him for it."

I think about her reasoning for a moment. She's right and I held respect for him too. On the other hand, I need to know more about him especially if I'm considering having any type of relationship with him.

Relationship? Getting a little ahead of yourself, aren't you?

"Hey, what's the matter?"

"Nothing, I was just thinking about what you said. There's one more thing I didn't tell you. I know you'll think I'm crazy, but I asked my friend the private investigator to do a background check on Landon." I look at the floor in shame.

"Really," She ponders this for a moment. "I don't think you're crazy and I'm glad to see that you were smart about this. I mean, I did drag you to a weird club. I would have doubts about getting involved with anyone from there too. So, what did you find out?"

"Nothing that you haven't already told me."

"I'll tell you what, I'll ask around a bit and see if I can find anything out," Haley offers.

"No." I practically shout. "You can't do that."

"Why not?"

"I don't want him to find out."

"Lexi. I know how to be discrete, okay?" she reassures me.

"Fine, but don't get caught asking too many questions," I beg her.

"I know, I know. I'll be careful, all right?"

"Fine. And Haley—thanks."

"You're welcome. I'm going to take off now, but you call me if you need me, okay?" She reaches over and hugs me before standing up.

I rise from the couch with her and follow her to the front door where she opens the door and spins to give me another squeeze.

"You take care of yourself. And, if you're asking me follow through with the divorce. As for Landon Miller I have a feeling that he could be something good for you."

I hold her tight.

"I'll consider it. See you later." I smile and wave as she walks down the front steps.

"See ya. Remember call if you need anything." She calls out as she strolls to her car.

"I will. Thanks for everything." I close the door.

CHAPTER 18

*A*rriving at the club, I'm scared, anxious and excited all at the same time. Thoughts of what tonight may bring have me questioning everything. *What does he want from me? What will we be after tonight? Does he want anything at all from me?* That thought scares me the most. Landon rejecting me never crossed my mind but why would it? After all, he is the one who set this evening up. *What if he is actively seeking new members for his club? What if this is all just a ploy to sell me a membership?*

Is there a membership?

How does this club even work?

Who classifies as a member?

What does it take to become a member?

If you are rejected, why are you rejected?

I have no idea and I really wish I thought to ask Haley some of these questions before letting her leave earlier. All these thoughts came crashing down around me as I step out of the limo and walk to the entrance of the club.

"Evening, Miss Shaw," the doorman greets.

"Evening, Riley," I reply, as he holds the door open for me.

I step inside the familiar room. Once inside, I notice the room is empty.

"Have a seat. Leroy will be with you shortly," Riley confirms.

"Thanks, Riley. Have a good night."

"You're welcome. Enjoy your evening as well." He closes the door.

I sit on the couch wondering why Leroy is coming to get me instead of Landon. Eagerness overwhelms me with the thoughts of spending more time with Landon. I pray that is the case that he wants to spend more time with me too. For Heaven's sakes he's the one who invited me—personally. Well, I suppose it wasn't exactly personally since it was Leroy who called but it sure felt like a personal invitation. Now here I sit waiting on Leroy, again.

The door across the room opens and Leroy steps in.

"Evening, Miss Shaw," he greets me.

"Evening, Leroy. Please, call me Lexi." I smile.

"Okay, Lexi, come with me. He's waiting for you," Leroy replies, returning the smile, as he stands at the elevator doors one arm holding them open.

Standing up I make my way over to him and to the waiting elevator.

"After you." He waves his free hand toward the open doors.

I enter the elevator, move right to the back and spin around to face the doors.

Leroy steps in, spins around and goes to the control panel displayed on the wall. He places his card in the slot at the top of the panel then presses the button displaying the letter 'L'.

The elevator begins to move, and we stand waiting silently. We stop moving and the doors open. Leroy steps to the doors, places his arm across the opening to keep them in place. He turns to me waving his other hand motioning me to exit.

I walk ahead exiting the elevator and stepping out of the way, so Leroy can exit too. I look around the waiting room of Landon's office remembering the last time I was in this room. Glancing around I notice the door to my right—a door that's hard to notice at first glance because it blends in with the wall—but it's a door I knew all too well. On my first visit I sat on the couch anxiously waiting for Haley to appear through that door.

As Leroy walks over and opens the door the butterflies in my stomach multiply and my hands begin to tremble. Hoping to hide my current problem I grasp my hands together in front of me and move through the doorway.

CHAPTER 19

Sitting behind his desk with his head down and his attention on paper work that is scattered around the desk is the man in question, the man who invaded my life from the first moment I saw him. The man who has captured my attention and now it seems he has captured my life.

I can't help the small twitching of a smile that is now trying to form on my lips. Landon, on the other hand, seems engrossed by whatever he is doing and hasn't even noticed my presence or the fact that I am now sitting across from him. *How can he be so oblivious to my presence when he literally moves every cell in my body? Do I have no effect on him at all?*

Finally, he glances up and smiles at me using his passive smile not quite the panty-dropping one I have witnessed on many occasions. His eyes remain fixed on mine giving me his undivided and making the butterflies in my stomach move even faster.

"Miss Shaw, lovely to see you again. I'm glad you accepted my offer to be here this evening." And there it is—that megawatt smile I have been waiting for.

"Thank you for offering, Mr. Miller," I reply, in a quiet voice I barely recognize.

"It's my pleasure, Lexi. As lovely as it is to see you I do believe in full disclose and I feel it is only fair to share with you the reason for my invitation. I do have an ulterior motive," he states, his face emotionless.

Damn it. I knew it. I had hoped he'd want me as much as I want him but deep down I knew that was a pipedream. I can feel myself deflating. My gaze hits the floor no longer unable to look at his beautiful face knowing he won't be mine. I should get up, excuse myself and walk out. I should state how wrong it is for him to get my hopes up only to dash them just as quickly. I should...

"I have a proposition for you. If you choose to accept this offer, our relationship will change dramatically. If you choose not to accept, well—" His voice trails off.

My ears perk up promptly hushing my internal dialogue.

"What is your offer, Mr. Miller?" I ask, my gaze able to meet his with a new found hope present.

"As you know I own this club and one of the reasons I do is to train new subs. I have been training new subs for many years now. It's kind of a—" he pauses to find the right words, "—mission of mine to ensure that subs are trained well. They leave here with a full knowledge of this lifestyle. By the time her training is done I expect her to be well informed on what is expected of her and what should never be allowed. If that makes any sense to you?" He finishes his statement, but his gaze remains fixed on mine.

I can feel the heat rising to my face under his intense glare and he hasn't even got to his proposal yet.

"I get it. You want to ensure the health and welfare of your subs?" I question, to clarify.

"Exactly, with one exception. They are not my subs, I only train them." He looks down at his desk but not before I catch the undertone of his last statement.

What does that mean they're not his subs? I am confused but before I'm able to question him further he continues.

"My offer is to train you. If you're willing? I know you are new to all of this." He waves his hand toward the door gesturing to the club on the other side, "and that it can be very confusing and hard to understand without proper guidance. So, that is what I am offering, to be your guide through the beginning stages of this lifestyle."

Shock. I am utterly shocked. My gaze never leaves his but now I know I look like a tomato because my face feels like it's on fire. *What does one say to an offer such as this?* My body is screaming yes—say yes—but my mind is shouting no—say no. *Is that what I truly want?* I'm not entire certain and beginning to panic.

Landon, on the other hand, sits extremely still gazing into my eyes while waiting for my answer. *How can I answer him when I have no clue what I want?*

"Yes."

What the hell?

Did that just come out of my mouth?

To further shock myself I continue, "I accept your offer."

What?

"Excellent," he replies.

Well, at least someone is happy with my sudden outburst. *What exactly did I sign up for?*

"There is some paper work we need to do first."

Landon gets up from his seat and makes his way to the filing cabinet. He digs through some drawers pulling out different sheets of paper and a file folder from the top of the cabinet.

Making his way around to my side of the desk he places his hand in front of me offering his hand. I take it immediately, placing my hand in his and get up from my seat.

He leads me to the opposite side of his office where there is another hidden door that looks like part of the wall. He opens the door, ushering me through it.

CHAPTER 20

Once I step over the threshold I'm certain the surprise on my face is quite evident as I open my eyes wide and glance around. Spectacular, is the word I would use to describe the living room we have just entered. There is a huge, black leather, circular couch that can accommodate at least twenty people strategically placed to dive the room in half. Nestled in front of the couch is a circular, hand crafted wooden coffee table. Beyond the table is a beautiful marble fireplace serving as the focal point of the room. To the right of the room there is a breakfast bar with four bar stools underneath the pass-through window to the kitchen. It's a state-of-the-art kitchen, with stainless steel appliances and cherry wood cupboards. I am speechless.

"Is—" I stumble over my words, "—this where you live?" I finally manage to choke out, as I glance around the room.

"No," he chuckles, "Well, I suppose I do part time, but

we'll get to that later. Come." He takes hold of my hand and leads me to the couch.

As I sit down I try to get comfortable as I continue to glance around the room. The beauty of this place is simply stunning. It's decorated in different shades of blue, light hues and tones, blending together in a unique way. Expensive appearing artwork lines the walls. Although it's decorated in dark colors, there is no lack of light. It doesn't feel as dark as it should considering there are no visible windows. There is no immediate explanation of natural light which leaves me with an unsettling feeling. There's also no indication that we are in a nightclub. No noise from the club can be heard. And this place looks as if it came out of designer magazine not your typical nightclub VIP room.

Landon reaches for a remote on the coffee table and presses a button.

On either side of the fireplace, the walls start to move as I watch with rapid fascination the horizontal panels turn sideways in unison revealing the outside world. The entire wall is a giant window, floor to ceiling, leaving a stunning view of the city. The entire scene takes my breath away.

Landon straightens out all the paper work on the coffee table holding the first sheet out to me. Quickly grasping the paper, I begin reading.

I read it over—twice, just to make certain I'm comprehend everything written. It's a contract of sorts between the two of us. It is a typical contract containing names, dates, times and places our arrangement will take place. All fields are left blank to be filled in by us.

I place the paper in my lap and glance up at Landon who is watching me intently. My mouth is suddenly dry, my mind working overtime, trying to figure out what to say.

Landon takes away that burden as he speaks.

"This is a contract between the two of us. It simply states when and where our time will be spent together and for how long," he states.

"Um… okay. So, when and where?" I ask quietly.

"Generally, I do all of my training here at the club." He waves gesturing around the room with his hand. "You would come here Friday night at six and stay until Sunday night at six. If that works for you?" He gazes into my eyes.

"Um… yes. That seems reasonable." As I say the words my mind goes into a frenzy.

Come again? Every weekend? He can't be serious? I gaze at his expression and there is no doubt he is very serious. *Doesn't he have a life? How can he do this every weekend?*

Why did I say yes so quickly? I have a life. Okay, I don't actually have a life, but so what? *Every weekend? Seriously?*

On a positive note, I would be with him every weekend.

Yes, but do you really want to be with him this way every weekend?

Insanity, that's what's happening here. I've gone completely insane. Which makes me question what is wrong with Landon knowing that he would want a crazy person around every weekend.

"Why...?" I ask, unwilling to ask what I really want to know.

"Why what, Alexandria?" he asks, glaring at me.

The intensity of his glare leaves me unable to think straight. It sets a fire raging throughout my body. *How am I so affected, simply by his stare?* Dropping my gaze to my lap as I try to regain a resemblance of composure. I need to calm down but that isn't happening.

"Why here?" I finally manage to squeak out, hiding the true question I am dying to ask—why me?

As the words leave my mouth I'm struck by another question. *Where does he live?* In all the research I've done about him nothing indicated where his residence is. I want to know but think better of asking. I will store that question away for a future date.

"That is what this place was designed for. My initial plan in building the club was to add a suite such as this. It has everything needed for training with the perfect set up. There was nothing overlooked. Everything here is safe and well maintained. Besides, I'd planned to spend most of my weekends here anyway, so it made sense at the time," he trails off as he retrieves the next piece of paper and hands it over.

The second sheet seems as legal as the first one. Having studied law in college, I knew this was drafted by a lawyer. Not that it would hold up in any court or anything, but it still felt official. Landon is thorough if nothing else.

Reading over the second page I realize it's an NDA. A Non-Disclosure Agreement. I'm kind of astounded for a moment, until I remember who I am sitting next to, which puts it back into perspective. No wonder information about this man is never leaked, which brings up another subject I want to ask about—his other trainees.

Surely, they knew that none of these papers would hold up in a court of law? If they spoke about Landon or their time together, in public, there would be nothing he could do about it.

"It's to ensure our privacy," he states in a harsh tone, as if he read my mind.

"I see." Although I really didn't, he must know these are meaningless.

I sign the document and decide to store those questions on my growing list.

Landon picks up a third piece of paper but holds onto it as his gaze roams over it.

My curiosity is beyond captivated wondering what this sheet can possibly contain, especially since he seems so reluctant to give it to me.

Landon shifts uncomfortably, glances up and looks me in the eye.

"Would you like a glass of wine?" he offers.

Really? That is what he wants to say to me? My mind is full of curiosity trying to figure out what the hell is on that third page. *What could he be so nervous about?*

"Um… sure," I answer in a shaky voice.

Landon gets up and goes to the kitchen to retrieve the wine. Unfortunately for me, he takes the third piece of paper with him. Seeing him so nervous scares the living daylights out of me. *What could he be so nervous about?* It must be bad. Really bad.

He returns with two glasses of wine and holding that sheet of paper that is now taunting me, close to his chest. As he sits down next to me closer than he was before with his leg pressed against mine.

CHAPTER 21

My gaze locks with his and we sit in silence. His gaze is too enticing, and I finally manage to break the connection by looking at the table in front of us instead. Picking up my wine I take a sip and wait for him to continue. I can feel his gaze on me the entire time and its uncomfortable being under such scrutiny.

Landon shakes his head and takes a sip of wine before speaking.

"There are many things we need to establish before we can begin your training. But before we continue with that can I ask you a question?"

He moves slightly folding one leg under himself, placing his elbow on the back of the couch and his head in his palm as he turns his full body towards me.

I glance sideways at him getting more nervous while he seems more relaxed. My heart is pounding so loud I could hear it in my ears and I know I can't answer so I simply nod.

"Why do you want to do this, Alexandria?" he asks, as his gaze shifts filling with enthusiasm.

As my name rolls off his tongue I can feel it everywhere from the tips of my toes to the top of my head. Heat runs through every part of me. I'm coming completely undone —fast. His question is almost forgotten as I glance at him. He sits so calmly waiting for an answer.

What the hell was the question? Oh yeah, why?

Good question. *Why did I want to do this?* I have no answer. None that I'm willing to reveal to him because I'm certain the truth will not go over well. I cringe hearing the answer in my head.

I'm here for you... I would do anything for you.

Yeah, that would do it—I'd be tossed out of here so fast my head would spin.

Tell him something.

My mind yells at me but I have nothing, no answers to give.

"It's not that complicated. Just tell me why?" he asks again, eager for an answer.

Still I have nothing as embarrassment washes over me. *How do I answer that? Why would anyone want to do this?* I have no idea. This whole relationship or whatever it is we are about to embark on is supposed to be built on honesty and trust. But there is no way I can be honest with him without ending it all before we have a chance to start.

"I... I don't know." I'm as honest as I can be while shifting my gaze back to my lap.

It really is the truth. I have no idea why. If this were

anybody but him I don't think I'd be here right now. I feel completely inadequate answering this way but that is all the truth I can reveal—for now.

"You don't know?"

I glance up to see his puzzled looking face.

"Okay, let me ask you this. How did you like the demonstrations? How did they make you feel?" he asks, curiosity dancing in his eyes.

I mull his question over in my mind for a moment.

The scene I witnessed with Haley had me shocked and confused. However, when I was with Landon I was definitely aroused. In fact, I don't remember ever feeling that aroused. Thinking of that night gets me all hot and flustered. I guess my only question would be, was it the scene that aroused me or was it him? I knew deep within my heart it was him but how can I explain that?

Peeking over at him he is watching me closely—a little too close for my comfort—but the expression on his face is a thoughtful one. It's as if he's searching for something in my face. *Is he trying to figure me out?* My only hope is that he doesn't because I need to figure out my own feelings before that flood gate opens.

"I guess, I was aroused." I instantly slap my hand over my mouth mortified at what has just slipped out.

Landon chuckles—actually, he laughs.

Embarrassed and anxiety ridden I stand from the couch, ready to leave.

He immediately stops laughing and grabs my arm.

"Sit," he commands.

I instantly drop back down still horrified by my

outburst and a little angered that I am following his commands so easily. The power he already possesses over me is becoming scary.

"I'm sorry for laughing. It's just that your expression was—" he pauses for a moment, "—perfect. You are so—" He looks down at his lap, "—innocent. And I know you hate that word but it's true. I find it very becoming," he says, flashing his million-dollar smile.

I sit staring at him as if he were an animal in the zoo. *How can he honestly find that becoming?* He makes no sense. He's a total contradiction. *How can he practice this lifestyle and find innocence becoming?*

"I don't understand," I blurt out.

"What's not to understand? You are like a clean slate. No bad habits to break, no annoying things that need to be changed. You will be the perfect trainee—" he waves his hand in front of me.

That's an interesting explanation and when he states it that way he's right, I am a clean slate. Training someone fresh and new who knows absolutely nothing is probably better than training someone who has been taught all the wrong things to begin with. Old dog, new tricks that kind of analogy. I peek over at Landon and he still seems amused which prompts my next question.

"It doesn't bother you... that I'm not..." I pause in search of the right wording. "...experienced in this sort of thing?" I finally ask.

"No, not at all. In fact, I prefer it that way, if I'm being completely honest. Breaking people of bad habits is not pleasant for me. Besides, it's a lot more fun when people have no idea what they are doing." He smirks. "And, that is part of the game to keep you guessing." His smirk turns slightly evil sending a shiver through me.

Reaching over I pick up my glass of wine and take a sip suddenly extremely parched. Placing the glass back on the coaster I place my hands in my lap and stare at them.

"Okay, let's move on," Landon says, handing me the infamous page three.

My hand shakes slightly as I take it from him. Glancing down the first thing I notice are the words hard/soft limits spread across the top. *Why was he so reluctant to give this to me?* After all, I already have a copy of his.

Reading the page further I become really confused, this is not the same page he had given me on my first night here. I guess my instincts were wrong and the sheet he gave wasn't his after all. It's similar but not the same.

"I know I gave you one of these already and you probably noticed some differences. But read it over then I'll explain," he offers.

I nod my head and read his list. First up, hard limits. They all seem the same except for—*is he kidding?* What the hell is this—no kissing?

What?

No touching him?

This must be a joke, right?

How can I not touch him? That's impossible considering what we are going to be doing. Reading further along I'm stunned. Along with no kissing and no touching are also no personal information exchanged and no love between the two participants.

How in the hell would you stop something like that?

This makes no sense what so ever. No wonder he has been so reluctant to give this to me. *How did he expect people to sign this?* I strain to remain still and not whip my head in his direction as I laugh at him. I'm struggling not to show any reaction at all but there is no doubt he is picking up on the inner battle raging inside of me at this moment.

Landon clears his throat and begins speaking. "Let me explain some of that stuff," he offers causally, while my inter voice begins laughing—hysterically.

My gaze remains on the paper. "Okay—"

"First, the no kissing and no touching. These are my hard limits, meaning you are never to initiate such acts. Only I can do that. Do you understand?" he asks, finally looking slightly embarrassed.

"Not really," I respond honestly.

"Okay. Let me see if I can clarify," he thinks for a moment. "If I want to kiss you, I will. If I want you to touch me, I'll tell you where you can. Other than that, its hands off for you. Does that clear it up?" he asks.

"I guess," I say, still unclear.

"No personal information is in place to let you know where you stand. You are a sub in training, that's it. Getting personal may lead to my next hard limit and I do realize putting that on paper seems—" he searches for words again, "—foolish. But it's there for my piece of mind," he finishes.

"You can't help something like that and having this piece of paper would make no difference how someone may feel," I offer.

"I realize that, Alexandria. And it's not there to confuse you. It's simply there to remind my trainees where they stand. Love, feelings of that nature will never happen, on my behalf anyways." He says the last part under his breath, almost as an afterthought not meant for my ears.

What does one say to such a ridiculous statement? What happened to this man to make him this way? How can he possibly know that he will never fall in love?

"Listen, it's there for your protection as well," he adds as an afterthought.

"What?" I ask, stunned by his statement. "What do you mean my protection? What do I need protecting from?" I ask confused.

"It's there to remind you and me that we have an agreement. It's to make certain that I train you to the best of my ability without feelings and emotions getting in the way. Do you understand?" he questions, as he places his hand on my arm.

Frankly no, I didn't understand a thing this man is saying.

"This is to offer you, or I, a way out if needed. If one of us found we were having these—types of feelings, we could simply use our safe word and that would be the end of it." he states, so casually.

"And you trust that whoever you train would do that?" I ask, astonished.

"Yes. You will find that this entire experience is built on trust. You don't know this yet, but if the trust isn't there. Or you are lacking in honesty, I will end this immediately. Without hesitation. It would do you good to remember that. I expect full disclosure and I give it in return." He commands. "Now there are a few more things on that list, but we'll get to them later. Let's discuss your list. Would you rather have a few minutes to fill it out or would you like to go over it point by point? It's up to you," he asks me pointedly.

CHAPTER 22

My mind is spinning like a top. This man confuses me to no end. There is nothing he does or says that gives me any indication of his true feelings. This whole contract is a farce and there's no way he can possibly believe that if we put it on paper it will make it true. It is hard to reconcile this Landon Miller with the multi-million-dollar businessman that the world knows. This is a man who probably signs contracts daily. Clearly, he must know all of this is hogwash.

"Point by point is fine. That way if I don't understand something you can explain it." My explanation is crap, I just want to hear his voice longer.

The silence envelops us as he stares at me a habit that is becoming quite unnerving. I finally figure out what he is trying to do—judge my reactions. I exert a lot of effort to keeping a straight face, giving nothing away because I don't want to reveal my feelings yet. Some of this stuff is really out there and I'm not ready to be so open. I know what is meant by full disclosure and when we start—whatever this is, I will provide him that. But for now, I need time away to prepare myself. Time and space away from him to think clearly.

Together we go through each point rather quickly which surprises me. I know a lot more than I had realized. Thank God for all those porno's my husband made me watch. After the list is finished I gulp down the last of my wine and relax back on the couch turning for the first time this evening to face Landon.

"Well now, that wasn't so hard was it?" he asks, with a sheepish grin.

"No, I guess not."

If you had asked me a month ago if I would be here discussing my limits with this man I would have laughed. But here I am, talking about nipple clamps, whips and other things that should be making me cringe. The odd thing is I'm not cringing. In fact, I'm extremely aroused and wish this paperwork was out of the way so we could get to the good stuff already. I suppose that's it—I've officially entered pervert territory. Welcome to the club.

I laugh at myself for that one. *Who would have thought Alexandria Lacy Shaw was a closet pervert?* Certainly not I. Or perhaps, it's the wine talking.

"What's so amusing?" he asks.

Oh shit, caught.

"Nothing," I smirk back at him.

"It doesn't look like nothing," he muses.

"Really, it's nothing."

He will not win. I will not tell him, no way, no how.

"When this—" He waves his hand over the paperwork, "—comes into effect, that answer will not suffice," he says.

I gulp—loudly—bringing a halt to my internal laughter. The things this man can do to me with just words is astounding.

"But, for today. Your secrets are safe." He smirks, once more.

Thank you, God because I really don't think I can explain that to him. I will however, remember that for the future. Never think anything I don't want him to know—in his presence anyways.

"Oh, how I would love to know what is in your mind right now?" he says, narrowing his eyes at me.

I thank God, once more that of his gifts—and there are many—mind reading is not one of them. I would literally die on the spot if he knew what I was thinking.

"Would you care for another glass of wine?" he asks, as he stands up.

"Yes, please."

Landon picks up our glasses and makes his way to the kitchen. I watch every move he makes. He's graceful considering his stature. He stands taller than six feet and is well built, not in the body builder type way but enough to look good from what is visible through his clothing. His movements seem automatic, smooth, unlike mine, which are well thought out and mostly clumsy. He glides his way back to the couch handing me my wine.

"Thank you."

"You're welcome, Alexandria." He smiles.

How can just saying my name make me whimper? Jesus, this

man is good. In that one statement he exudes lust, desire, yearning and more than anything, sex. *How the hell is he able to do that?* Anytime he says my name my body stands at attention and my heart pounds relentlessly. If I sit here much longer I'm going to jump him. There's no doubt about that.

"So, there are a few more papers to get through," he says, as he hands me page number four.

There is a lot more to this than I had originally thought. I take the page and begin reading. Just when I thought there were no more surprises, boom—a bomb explodes in my head as he hits me with another one. This page is by far the worst of them all and reading it sends a chill through me instantly.

This page is all about my transition from him to my real Dom once my training is finished. My real Dom. *Shit!* I think about that for a minute. *Do I want a real Dom?* Yes, but I always thought that would be Landon's role. He is making it perfectly clear that he will not be my Dom or anything else.

This charade has gone on long enough. I have no intentions of getting another Dom. I should tell him thanks, but no thanks. I should just get up and leave. However, I don't do either of those things. Instead I sit staring at the paper willing it to go away.

The funny thing about that is it does—disappear. Landon snatches it from my hands and places it back into the folder and pulls out yet another sheet of paper completely ignoring the paper about my transition to another Dom.

Hesitantly, I take it from him scared to find out what it is. As I slowly read the document my insides perk up a bit. It's an application for membership to the club. It's a relief from all the other thoughts that are running through my mind to see such a simple document.

Placing the paper on the coffee table I begin filling it out.

Landon places his hand over mine to get my attention.

"Just sign it, love. I'll fill out the rest later," he states.

Don't think I missed his term of endearment, because I didn't. Perhaps, he says that to all his trainees. I will have to store that information away for future thought.

"Okay." I sign the bottom and hand it back to him.

"All right. We're almost finished," he says with a smile while gathering the last few papers.

I quietly thanked the heavens because it is becoming rather warm in here and Landon isn't helping the matter as he scoots closer to me. His thigh is now touching mine and it is driving me insane.

He holds the last few pages between us as he speaks.

"The rest of these are explaining my duties toward you. How I will keep you sane, healthy and safe at all times. It goes on to ensure my commitment to you throughout your training and how I will never push you past your limits," he explains and then moves so close to me that his breath is in my ear. "It also states that I'm tied to you until I feel your training is finished," he whispers making me shiver. He pulls back a bit to finish. "So, you'll need to initial these pages." He hands them to me.

I immediately put them on the coffee table and initial

them all handing them back. He stares into my eyes for a long moment before talking again.

"That's all. Its official, your training will begin Friday at six," he says, with a wink.

I know that I shouldn't sign anything without consulting a lawyer first, but seriously, as if I would take these papers to a lawyer. *How embarrassing would that be?* The truth is these documents are worthless in the legal world. He knows it, I know it, all of this is just a formality to make all parties feel better, I suppose.

Landon scoots back down the couch, gathers all the paperwork, puts it in the file folder and places it neatly on the coffee table. He stands up extending his hand to me and I immediately place mine in his. He pulls me to stand in front of him.

"Let me give you the grand tour," he says, stepping around the couch towards the kitchen, pulling me behind him.

Beside the breakfast bar is an opening that leads down a hallway.

*a*s we move through the opening of the hallway Landon stops and waves his hand at the first opening on the left.

"This is the kitchen. I will prepare dinner every Friday night at six. For the rest of the weekend it is your responsibility."

He turns continuing further down the hallway before he stops and opens the first door on the right.

Meanwhile, my mind is back in the kitchen thinking about the fact that he cooks. This man is too good to be real.

"This is your room. It's pretty plain so you can decorate as you see fit," he says with a smile.

"What do you mean decorate?" I ask to confirm.

"Paint, comforters or sheets, stuff like that. Let me know what you would like, and I'll see to it," he simply says.

"Oh, I'm sure this will be fine," I counter, as I walk in and look around.

The room is huge, bigger than my living room and the focal point of the room is a massive bed covered with the warmest looking purple comforter I've ever seen. With about a dozen designer pillows neatly placed along the top.

Along the right side of the wall is a door and beside that a tall, dark wooden chest of drawers. On the wall above of the chest of drawers is an elegant black and white photograph of a woman who is naked, kneeling with her back to the camera, hands behind her back and head bowed. Her long blonde braid running down the middle of her back. The contrast is stunning and if we were in an art gallery I just might approve of the artwork. But in this room, it leaves me uncomfortable. *Is this one of his former subs?*

"There's a full bath through that door," he points to the door on the right, "and a walk-in closet through that door," he points to the left. "Don't worry about bringing anything with you on Friday night. You'll have everything you need here."

Wait! What does he mean by that?

I wonder as I spin around to face him.

"I don't understand what you mean, I'll have everything I need. You mean clothes and stuff?" I ask, bewildered.

"Yes, Alexandria. We are in the middle of my club. We will be making appearances there from time to time and you need to be dressed appropriately. That closet will be full when you return with the clothes I approve of." He states this like it's the most obvious thing in the world. No big deal.

This is a very big deal. I have enough clothing of my own and there is no reason for him to buy me things. I am not happy about this but not sure how to state that to him either, so I keep silent. Not one of my finest moments I'll have you know.

"Everything you need for the bathroom will be provided too. So, no need to bring anything for that, either."

Well, this is becoming ridiculous. *How can he presume I will be okay with all of this?* And just as I'm about to protest, tell him how irrational he is sounding, he continues.

"Come, I'll show the rest of the suite." He stretches his hand out to me, once again.

Instead of protesting, instead of telling him how truly ludicrous all of this is, I simply place my hand in his and follow him. I should've known in that moment how wrong it was of me to blindly follow this man who I know nothing about. I should have asked more questions. I should have asked for time to think over everything he was offering without his influence.

Instead, I let him lead me through the hallway to another door on the right. He swings it open and stands aside, wanting me to go first.

"This is my playroom," he says, quietly.

I walk forward, dropping his hand and going to the middle of the room to take a long look around. It isn't far off from what I'd envisioned. Its painted dark blue and black and the lighting, oddly enough is bright just like the living room. On the wall to my right are two doors that are closed. On my left is a wall full of whips, canes and belts hanging on it. The wall in front of me has a huge king size bed with blue and black pillows and a blue comforter covering it. A tall dresser is placed next to it and on the wall above that is a black box concealing whatever is inside.

Turning around I notice a large X in the corner and another chest of drawers next to the door.

Landon stands in the doorway watching me closely. I'm not sure what he sees but suddenly he is smiling. The thing about his smile is you can't help but smile back.

"This will probably be the only time you will smile like that in here." He motions around the room with his hand. "Come," he says, as he outstretches his hand to me.

Once again, I immediately take his hand after missing the contact and realizing how comfortable I am with my hand in his. It feels natural to be holding his hand and I find myself wondering how it makes him feel to.

We walk across the hall to the next door which Landon swings open. Inside is a laundry room.

"Self-explanatory really, but if you need linens or towels, this is where they'll be," he states. "I have a house-keeper who comes during the week." He looks at me sheepishly. "She's very discrete," he whispers.

I nod my head at him.

"She won't see you, or know who you are," he adds, trying to reassure me.

He simply bows his head and closes the door turning down the hall the way we came. He stops at the first door across from mine and opens it hesitantly.

"This is my room." he turns to face me.

I stand still waiting for an invitation. Suddenly, he seems uncomfortable but waves his hand motioning me through the door.

I hesitate only a moment before walking in. His room is just as breath taking as the rest of this place. Decorated in the same dark blue—he certainly has a thing for blue. A huge king size, four-poster bed with a navy-blue comforter and more designer pillows dominate the space. Sitting on either side of the bed are two nightstands both with reading lamps perched on top but only one has books piled on it and a pair of reading glasses on the stack. It's quite apparent that only one stand is in use currently which gives me an overwhelming sense of relief. On both sides of the two nightstands are doors. I'm assuming one is the bathroom and the other a closet.

On the opposite side of the room is a fireplace nestled into the wall and made of the same marble as the one in the living room. A huge TV screen hangs above stealing most of the attention. Surrounding the fireplace is a black leather couch and two-winged back chairs which appear as the perfect spot to sit and read but are also placed strategically to enjoy the fire.

The room is meant to be warm and cozy, but something is missing that makes it seem cold and sterile and I can't seem to figure out what that missing something is.

Landon walks to the door next to the unused nightstand.

"That is the bathroom." He points to the door. "And that is the closet." He points across the bed to the other door.

He walks back to stand in front of me.

"You're never to come in here unless I tell you otherwise. Okay?" His voice takes on a harsh tone making me wonder what he is hiding. And by the expression on his face he's hiding something.

"Okay."

Landon steps around me and begins to head out the door. I follow along behind him noticing that he doesn't take my hand this time. His whole demeanor has changed, and I can't figure out what happened.

CHAPTER 24

*H*e turns back towards the playroom and my heart skips a beat. It isn't until that moment I notice the door at the end of the hall which Landon halts in front of and waits for me. When I arrive next to him, he opens the door to reveal a garage. I am astounded wondering how there could be a garage in here when we are not on the ground level and inside a club no less.

"This is where you will park when you arrive. No one will know you are here. Unless of course, I want them to know," he states.

I peek up at him a surprised expression no doubt plastered across my face.

"As with the NDA no one will have knowledge of our arrangement. Again, unless I want them to," he says with a smile.

Things are beginning to click in my mind, an understanding as to why he feels the need to train subs. He likes control.

As I walk into the garage a man comes strolling toward us from the opposite corner of the room startling me.

"Evening, Mr. Miller," the man greets.

"Evening, Lawrence," Landon returns the greeting, all business in his tone.

Lawrence, an older gentleman perhaps mid-forties, casually strolls up to stand in front of us. His demeanor is all business with a stern approach reminding me of a of a cop or security person.

"Anything I can do for you, Mr. Miller?" Lawrence asks.

"Yes, please give me five minutes," Landon demands.

"Sure, I'll be back in five." The man nods, then walks back to the door he came through.

Landon turns to me.

"Can you wait here for a minute?" he asks, his tone softer.

"Sure."

Landon turns and heads back in to the suite. I remain still and glance around space. There are three cars in the garage, a sports car of some sort, a black Mercedes, I believe, and a huge black SUV. The man has way too many cars that is quite apparent. The garage, like the rest of this place, is neat, clean and well maintain.

Little time has passed before Landon comes back holding my purse, jacket and a big brown envelope. I look at him confused.

Lawrence makes another appearance at that moment.

"I'll need the keys to the crossfire," Landon snaps, rather rudely if you ask me.

"Right away, Mr. Miller." Lawrence disappears through

the door, again. He comes back, handing Landon a set of keys.

Landon presses the remote lock button and pulls me towards the little sports car. I guess we're leaving. I wish he would inform me of what is happening. He simply opens the passenger door and ushers me inside handing me my purse and jacket then closing the door for me.

He proceeds around to the driver's side, gets in, places the envelope on his lap and starts the engine. He pulls the car forward until we come to a wall. Landon presses a button on his visor and the wall opens. He continues to drive, and we go down a circular slope, much like you would see in a public parking garage. When we reach the bottom, we are confronted by another wall. He pushes another button and the wall opens. He drives forward, and we are now outside pulling onto a street.

As he drives, Landon hands me the envelope he had placed on his lap.

"You will find all instructions and anything else you will need to know before Friday in there," he states.

I stare at the envelope almost afraid to open it.

"I would like you to come to the club on Thursday night for your last—" he thinks for a moment, "—night of freedom for a while," he says with a smirk. "After Friday, you'll be limited," he grins. "So, come and have some fun on Thursday night."

"Okay," I say, a little surprised by his offer.

The only word that has made it passed my lips in the last hour has been 'okay'. My vocabulary is quite extensive but for some reason I can't seem to find any words for all that I am feeling. I'm certain Landon is beginning to think I am a little slow.

"I would like to come on Thursday for my last fling, as you so eloquently put it," I say, smiling.

"Fling—" he pauses for a moment. "Interesting word," he says, in a harsh tone.

His reaction and tone startle me. *Is he mad?* He must know I am joking.

Yeah, like he knows you well enough to figure that out.

Say something... anything... make it right.

"I didn't mean it like—"

Landon cuts me off.

"It's all right, Alexandria. I knew what you meant," he says, giving me his signature smile.

Before I realize where we're going Landon is pulling into my driveway and getting out of the car.

At first, I wonder what he is doing as my stomach drops. My hope soars thinking he might want to come in but before I have time to consider the possibility, he is at my door, pulling the handle open. He extends his hand confidently and I let him help me out of the car, although, I am quite capable of doing it on my own.

Landon walks me to my front door and hesitates on the porch.

"Well, I'll see you on Friday," Landon says.

"Will you not be there on Thursday?" I ask, startled by his statement. If he's not going to be there I probably won't waste my time going.

"I'll be around but not certain I'll see you—" His gaze directly on me, "—business to take care of."

Before I can say anything, he adds more.

"Remember that you now represent me. You better be on your best behavior," he adds with a grin.

I can't tell if he is joking or not.

"You'll never have to worry about that."

"Very well. I'm glad to hear it." He reaches down takes a hold of my hand, brings it up to his lips, and presses a kiss on the back of it. "Have a good evening, Alexandria."

"You too, Landon."

Landon walks away as I stand and admire the view. He turns to me before getting in his car.

"I'll see you Friday," he reminds me.

"Six o'clock, sharp." I smile.

He gives me his signature smirk before he gets in his car and backs out of my driveway. I stand frozen on the front porch watching his car disappear.

Sighing heavily, I turn and walk in the house. This night did not go at all how I planned. To make matters worse I didn't have dinner and now I'm starving.

CHAPTER 25

*B*y Monday I'm a nervous wreck. No, nervous wreck is an understatement because my feelings are all over the place.

I'm scared but curious, apprehensive but thrilled and I can't imagine how on earth I will last managing all these feelings until Friday. I want to prepare but haven't the slightest idea how to do that. *What could you possibly do to prepare for something like this?*

My mind is a flurry imagining all kinds of scenarios that could play out in Landon's playroom. I've seen two demonstrations and for the most part they were very arousing. On the other hand, this venture involves forms of punishment, a notion that is completely foreign to me. Since I've never seen what would be considered punishment I have no idea what it may entail. I've never been hit in my entire life. Growing up my parents didn't believe in corporal punishment, so I was never spanked—ever.

Here, in the safety of my home, the visions of what may

happen this weekend terrify me. Especially the thought of being hit with an object. There are plenty of people who engage in this lifestyle. *Honestly, how bad can it be?*

The thought crossed my mind to call Haley, just to ask her opinion but for some reason I just can't bring myself to tell her. Yes, she is my best friend. And yes, she of all people should understand but there's still a small voice in my mind instructing me to leave her out of this. While my brain scrambles with all these thoughts, I remember the envelope Landon had given me last night.

After retrieving it from my hallway table, I go back to the couch and sit down preparing to go through all the documents. The first document is our arranged times and dates. I'm still amazed that he wants to do this every weekend. Placing the first page on the coffee table I look at the next one, which is the NDA he had me sign. I hold back my laughter thinking about how useless these documents truly are. The third and fourth are our lists of limits. I glance over my list and my face burns as I focus on some of the things I've agreed to try. I pause wondering what I was thinking when I made this list. Although, I knew exactly what I was thinking, I truly wasn't thinking straight. When I am around Landon all coherent thoughts fly right out the window. He has the ability to render me useless which is bound to be very dangerous, but I can't seem to find it in myself to care.

Flipping to the next page I come across the infamous page titled Transfer of Dom. The page makes me shiver. The thought of being passed off to someone like some sort of business arrangement, merchandise or property makes me nauseous. If I tell him not to worry about transferring me to another Dom it will only have him wonder, why I would want to be trained in the first place. If he knew the truth, he would never consider training me.

As I sit staring at the document I want to forget its existence. I would burn it if that would make it disappear. The truth is that it does exist and no matter how hard I try to wish it away it won't work. It is here, taunting me, and deep down I know that somehow this little piece of paper will be my demise.

Pushing that thought out of my head I place the offending document to the bottom of the pile quickly knowing my heart will break from its sheer presence.

Peeking at the next sheet of paper I release a gust of air I didn't realize I was holding as I stare at my application for the club. I'm now a full-fledged member of this exclusive club and I can't be more thrilled about it. This means I will always have a connection to Landon even in this small way. On the off chance our little arrangement doesn't work out knowing I can still see him brings a smile to my face. I realize it's foolish to think this way and I am digging a huge hole of regret but just can't seem to care.

The last couple of pages are promises by Landon. They reveal all the things he will do while I'm undergoing my training. The detail provided in these papers tells me how serious he takes his position. Nothing is overlooked on this sheet of paper right down to the smallest of things, such as, providing me with bathing supplies. I must hand it to the guy he's certainly meticulous. Along with his promises are the ones I have made like learning different positions for him and hand signals. Some I need to learn before our first session.

Glancing them over I'm certain in my ability to memorize them by Friday night.

After I finish reading all the documents I place them back in the envelope for safekeeping.

Leaning my head far back on the couch I'm left with one thought—Friday night can't come fast enough. *How will I ever make it through the entire week feeling this elated?*

CHAPTER 26

By Wednesday I'm a bundle of nerves as I return home from shopping and spot the light on my answering machine flashing. I retrieve a message from my investigator friend asking me to call him when I have the chance.

I immediately dial his number and after three rings, he finally answers.

"How's it going, Lexi?"

"Good, good. Tell me you have more information?" I beg, a little needy.

"Wow, anxious aren't we?" he inquires, while laughing.

"Give it up. Tell me what I want to know, please?"

"All right. All right. It's nothing huge. It's a little weird actually, but I thought you'd want to know."

"Tell me," I snap.

"He dropped out of college his first year," he begins.

"What?"

"I said he dropped out suddenly after one year of

college." He pauses before continuing. "There's no reason. None that I could find. There's nothing. I mean it Lexi, there's absolutely nothing," he finishes and remains quiet.

I ponder this for a moment almost forgetting he is on the phone.

"Lexi? Did you hear me?"

"Yeah. Sorry, I'm just thinking."

"I'm sorry I couldn't find out anything more, but everyone involved is quite tight-lipped about this," he offers.

"It's all right. Don't worry about it. This information is good. Thank you."

"No problem. Anything for you, dear. I'll keep my ear to floor for anything else," he offers.

"Thanks again. I'll talk to you soon." I hang up.

I begin to wonder what all of this means. I can't for the life of me think of why Landon would leave college after only one year. It couldn't have been a death or sickness in the family, this would have been public. So what other reason could there have been? After much consideration I realize that I'm not going to figure this out on my own and give up, turning in for the night.

As I close my eyes I'm still uncertain if I will make an appearance at the club tomorrow night. The week has been long, and I want to see Landon but knowing there's a possibility that I won't see him tomorrow night has me reconsidering my plan. I fade off to sleep with that unanswered question roaming my mind.

CHAPTER 27

Standing in front of the full-length mirror in my bedroom fully dressed and ready to leave the house, I've decided to go. Looking at my reflection in the mirror I'm still on the fence about my decision. I have taken into consider that I've lost my mind, but I still hold out hope that this will bring me closer to Landon. Stupid really but I can't help praying that somehow, he will see me as more than a trainee. I know the reality of that happening is slim but if there is a chance, even the slightest chance that he may feel more for me then I must take the risk. What I have realized is that I can't just walk away from him, not at this point. Somehow, he has maneuvered his way into my life and I can't just walk away—not yet. I owe it to myself to find out what can become of this.

Leaving the house, I opt to take a cab to the club again. I always feel that if there is a possibility of drinking I refuse to drive. It just makes sense to take away the temptation of having a vehicle there at the end of the night.

Everything goes as smoothly as it had on my other arrivals. Leroy greets me tonight and escorts me to the bar again. He explains to me that Landon is very busy tonight and will most likely not be able to stop by. He tells me to have fun and that anything I want is on the house. He also tells me that there is a demonstration I really should see and what room it is in before he bids me goodnight.

So here I sit at the bar sipping my drink wondering once more, 'what the hell am I doing here?' Oh, right, I'm here to see someone who is too busy to see me. That thought leaves me feeling empty, but I suppose it just re-enforces the contracts Landon insists on having. The problem with the contract is I've already broken it and I'm going to continue to break it because I already have strong feelings for the man that I am not being honest about.

Picking up my drink I glance around the room. There are plenty of people here tonight. In fact, it is rather surprising just how many are here on a work night.

"Is something special going on tonight?" I lean into the bar to ask the bartender.

"Actually, there is supposed to be some expert on Kinbaku tonight in one of the demonstration rooms. I've heard he's really good," the bartender replies with a smirk.

"What is Kinba...?" I attempt to ask but can't quite make out the word.

"Kin...bak...u." The bartender sounds out the word. "It's a type of rope binding. You should check it out," the bartender answers, flashing me a smile.

"Maybe I will."

"You should go soon." He glances at his watch. "It's

going to start in twenty minutes and the room will fill up quickly."

"Which room is it in?"

"Just go out that door turn left and it's the third door on the right." He points in the direction of the exit across the room.

"Thank you." I finish my drink and hop off my stool. "I'll see you later," I call out, as I turn for the door.

I walk out the door, turn to my left and notice a crowd of people already making their way into the room. I follow the crowd making my way along the back wall. As more people pile in I move deeper into the room toward the left side wall.

I lean up against the wall and wait patiently. I'm not sure what this demonstration will consist of but with this many people here to see it I know this Kinbaku must be special.

Peering around the room it doesn't escape my attention how different all these people are. Through my previous visits it's obvious who is a Dom and who is a submissive. This time I'm scrutinizing how the Dom's are interacting with their subs. It is interesting to witness but having no idea what the etiquette is in a situation such as this I try not to look at any one couple for too long.

From my viewpoint most of the couples are beautiful. Their movements with each other are incredible and the attention being paid to each other seems very loving. To an outsider being collared and leashed would not be considered loving but somehow within the walls of this club these couples do not portray what would be considered the standard vision of Master and Slave. The pride being displayed by both parties is clear as both working hard to please the other, giving to each other so freely. Love is the last thing I thought I would see in this kind of lifestyle but here it is displayed in many couples.

My attention falls to the front of the room where there's a stage set up. In the middle of the stage is a woman who is sitting on her knees with her hands behind her back and her head down. Judging from her position I'm certain she's the sub for the demonstration but there's no one else on the stage with her. She's a beautiful woman from what I can see of her with long blonde hair pulled back into a ponytail. She's perfectly still resembling a statue only the rise and fall of her chest let me know she's alive. She's completely naked except for the thick black collar around her neck. She's a remarkable sight.

The room suddenly falls silent as the crowd parts and a man quickly makes his way to the stage. He pauses to take inventory of the equipment laid out on the table. From my view point he is only visible from behind and he is dressed in old black tattered jeans and a black t-shirt that clings to him like a second coat of skin, showing off his muscular back. There is something oddly familiar about him.

I watch in awe as he re-arranges everything on the table. He spins around to face the audience.

Shock courses through me when the man on the stage standing next to one of the most beautiful women I've ever seen, is revealed as my new Dom.

Landon reaches down and strokes the woman's cheek with the back of his hand. He begins speaking to the crowd, but I can't comprehend a word he is saying. All I can see is his hand running through her ponytail repeatedly. It's such a loving gesture that leaves me feeling distraught.

The sub never once falters, remaining perfectly still and I wonder how she can do that as his presence envelopes her. I watch her closely for any signs of his effect on her. It takes a minute and you would have to be looking extremely closely but I can make out her subtle movement. Her breathing is ragged.

My heart leaps as my chest tightens. My stomach churns when Landon places his hand on her shoulder and she takes a deep breath to steady herself, nothing anyone would notice useless they were paying close attention.

The sub stands from her spot and moves toward the table where all of Landon's equipment is laid out for his demonstration. He is standing next to the table gathering the ropes in his hands.

He is still talking to the crowd but again my brain can't seem to make out what he is saying. I am too busy watching his hands. He begins placing the ropes strategically around her with purpose but what I'm focused on is the way he is touching her.

From my vantage point every movement is fluid, purposeful. Honestly, it looks sensual. His concentration never falters, and he seems very passionate about what he is doing. The attention Landon is paying to this woman is disturbing and I'm battling an inner demon who hasn't made an appearance in my life in years—jealousy. I am extremely jealous and can feel the heat rising to my face as

I burn with jealousy. I know one thing for certain—I've must leave this room, and fast, before I do something very stupid.

I begin to make my way along the wall towards the door refusing to even glance at the stage again because if I do Lord knows what I will see or do. I keep my eyes on the door willing myself to move faster but also trying not to bring attention to myself.

Finally, I reach my destination and step into the hallway taking a deep breath of air. My chest hurts as I let out the breath.

CHAPTER 28

I stumble my way back to the bar where I am greeted by the same bartender.

"Did you enjoy the demonstration?" he asks, with a smirk.

It's in that moment I know he knew exactly who was giving the demonstration. I wonder if it was Landon's plan for me to attend his performance.

"Not really," I answer.

"Really? From what I've heard it's one of the better demonstrations. People come here specifically to watch it. What didn't you like?" he asks, with an amused expression on his face.

I begin to wonder what the hell is going on here. If Landon truly wanted me to see his demonstration, he would have asked me to come himself. With the bartender acting all weird, I wonder who's really behind me seeing that demonstration in the first place.

"Too crowded. It was difficult to see anything." I choose not to indulge this conversation any longer.

"That's too bad. Maybe next time you'll get a better view," he says, as he waggles his eyebrows.

Does he know that I am Landon's newest trainee? Has Landon told everyone at the club about our arrangement? That doesn't seem his style at all. He doesn't appear to be the type to go around telling that sort of information. Something isn't right here but for the life of me I can't figure out what it is.

"Yeah, maybe next time." I pick up the drink he has placed in front of me.

I spin around on my bar stool putting an end to this conversation. This whole night isn't at all what I had planned and for the first time I feel uncomfortable being here. *Did I make a mistake accepting Landon's offer? Why do I get the feeling that there's so much more going on in this club?* Unexpectedly, I want to leave. I'm no longer content sitting on this bar stool—in this club.

The feelings coming to the surface while I watched Landon with another woman surprised me. Those are feelings I haven't felt since high school and they weren't enjoyable then either. I can't understand what is happening but it's completely out of character for me to be jealous. I am a strong, confident woman with no reason to be jealous. Besides, Landon made it clear that he never dates his subs —ever. *So, why can't I shake the feeling that she seems more than a sub?*

Crazy, that's what I've become—crazy. This whole experience is making me question my sanity. All the thoughts, all the questions and all the things new to me are just too confusing to deal with while here—in this place. I need to go home where I can sort through everything properly, without any distractions and decide whether this lifestyle is something I really want. Perhaps, Landon was right all along and I'm just too naïve for all of this.

I stand up from my stool but before I have a chance to leave a man approaches me.

"How's it going?" he asks, with a smile plastered across his face.

I look at him for a moment because he seems familiar to me but I'm having a hard time placing him.

"Good, thank you."

"You don't remember me, do you?" he asks, his smile faltering slightly.

"I was just trying to place where I knew you from."

"I met you here once. It was a couple of weeks ago. You've probably forgotten, it was just briefly," he explains.

"Oh yes. I remember, your name is—" I pause trying to recall his name, "—Jackson?"

"Jason. But close." He smiles brighter.

"Right, Jason. Sorry," I answer, feeling foolish.

"Don't worry about it. Like I said, it was brief," he says.

I smile as I take a sip of my drink unsure of what to say.

"So, are you having fun this evening?"

"Sure." I shrug my shoulders.

"That doesn't sound like you're having fun. It's demonstration night. Have you seen any?" he asks.

"Only one. A rope demonstration," I offer.

"Ah, yes, Landon. He's very good with ropes," he replies.

The tone he uses kind of disturbs me but before I can think too much about his response he continues.

"There are many more happening tonight. You should see some others," he states.

"I guess."

I don't know how to answer this man. It isn't that I feel uncomfortable around him but there is just something about him I can't put my finger on. Maybe it's this place. Being here and knowing what kind of lifestyle these people live is probably making me over think everyone and everything.

"You know they are having a really cool one downstairs in about five minutes. Would you care to join me?" he asks.

I hesitate a moment, not sure if I should. *Do I trust this man?* Now I'm really starting to think I'm insane and paranoid too. I don't know what my problem is. I'm in a club, surrounded by tons of people. *What the hell is my problem?*

"Sure, I'll come." I slide off my stool.

I glance around the bar to say good-bye to the bartender but he's no longer there.

Jason stands next to me motioning for me to walk ahead of him, which I do. We walk out into the hallway and I wait for him to guide me the rest of the way.

CHAPTER 29

As we walk along the corridor I'm feeling more at ease and decide to find out who this man is.

"Do you know, Mr. Miller? From the club?" I inquire.

"Landon? No." He stops walking to stand in front of the elevator. "Landon and I were college roommates," he explains.

"Really? So, you know him pretty well then?" I ask, curiosity etched in my voice.

"Oh yeah, we go way back." He pauses before walking into the now open elevator. I follow along. "He's a good guy," is all he offers.

"Yeah, he seems like he is."

The doors close and we begin our decent. Although this man knows Landon personally, I get the idea he isn't being completely honest. He has an edge to his voice at the mention of Landon's name. There is something about him that isn't quite right but again, I can't figure it out.

This place sure plays with my instincts. Usually I'm

very good at judging people but being in this place I feel inadequate. It's hard to gather my wits about me. Feeling this way is very unnerving—ridiculous. After all this is a very exclusive club, I mean, they don't let just anyone in here. I'm certain none of these people are murderers or serial rapists or anything like that. I know Landon is very particular about who he gives memberships to his club.

The elevator dings announcing our floor. I step out into another hallway.

"This way." Jason motions to me and I step forward and begin walking down a long hallway with him following behind. In this moment there are things I should've noticed, things that should've sent me the other way, but hindsight really is 20/20 as they say and in this moment, it just didn't occur to me.

"It's the last door on the left. It should be open," he says. "This demonstration doesn't start for a bit."

I walk to the last door and step inside with him following right behind. I walk further into the room and glance around. Immediately, I notice the room doesn't resemble the other demonstration rooms. I have only seen one other room that looks like this one and that is Landon's personal playroom. My heart begins to beat a little faster, but I take a deep breath in an attempt to control it.

I hear the door close and a lock click into place. My heart now drops into my stomach as I try to breathe. Quickly, I gather myself as best as I can and turn to face Jason.

"What are you doing?" I ask in a shaky voice.

He stands with his back to me and his hands against the door. He doesn't move at first. Slowly, he turns to me, giving me a malicious smile.

I can feel all the color drain from my face and my body begins to tremble.

"I just wanted to get you alone." He steps toward me as I step back. "You are very beautiful, you know." He smiles again, an unpleasant smile.

"Um, thank you?" I respond, more like a question then an answer. "I think you have the wrong impression here."

"No, I don't think I do," he says, without the smile this time.

My brain is spinning as I attempt to figure out what to do or how to get out of here. Several scenarios run through my mind and my brain is yelling at me to think, think, think—damn it. I need to get out of here—quickly. As the panic sweeps through my entire body I suddenly feel very calm.

"I'm sorry if I've given you the wrong impression. But this—" I motion around the room. "—is not something that I am interested in."

"Oh, I'm sure you're interested. Otherwise, you wouldn't be here." He takes another step toward me.

I take another step backward bumping against something as I do. I place my hands behind me and realize it is some sort of table. I'm trapped.

This can't be happening. This can't be happening. I can't let this happen. That is the mantra running through my mind as my brain is still telling me to think.

"Well, you brought me here under false pretenses."

"I wasn't talking about this room," he says, smiling maliciously again.

"The club? I've only been coming here to see if this lifestyle is for me. I still haven't decided," I ramble, still trying to figure a way out of this.

"Well, I can help you decide," he says, as he closes the distance between us.

"I'm not sure that's a good idea."

I'm saying anything that comes to mind in an attempt to stall because I still haven't come up with a plan to escape.

"Why? Because you belong to Landon?" he asks.

"No. I... don't belong... to Landon." My voice stutters and my entire frame shakes.

It's at this moment I believe I've blown any chance of walking out of this room of my own freewill. I'm a terrible liar and know he'll see right through me.

He reaches his hand out and places it on my cheek.

I freeze as he runs his thumb along my bottom lip. Somehow, I square my shoulders and slap his hand away from my face.

"There's no reason to lie. I know you belong to him," he says, as reaches out again. "That's oaky. He won't mind if we have a little fun," he laughs.

I slap his hand away again and try to walk around him, but he grabs me around the waist pushing me back against the table.

He brings his face inches from mine and licks his lips.

I freeze once more still trying to work out my best option as a plan forms in my mind.

"I think he might," I answer, while bringing my knee up to his groin—hard.

He falls to the floor yelling in pain and calling me every name in the book. I push him further down as I step over him and run for the door. Reaching the door my hands fly out in front of me feeling for the handle before I quickly realize there isn't one. I stop my hand movements sharply and look up and down but all I see is a keypad. I bang on the door with both my hands and close my eyes. I can hear him laughing in the background.

"You didn't think you could get away that easy. Did you?" He laughs harder.

I feel the tears run down my face, as I realize I am truly trapped. His laughter is like nails on a chalkboard grating on my nerves and making my panic state peek.

"Don't worry babe. I've got all night," he says, laughing that manic laugh.

"What do you want?" I turn to face him.

"What do you think I want?" He smiles sending shivers down my spine.

"Why?" I sob a little. "Why me?"

"I told you. You're beautiful. I have an appreciation for beautiful women," he steps in front of me again. "I like to bring pleasure to beautiful women." He comes face to face with me wearing an evil smile and a look of determination in his eyes.

"Please—don't," I beg him.

"Don't what, honey?"

"Please don't—hurt me."

"Oh sweetheart. I'm not going to hurt you. Trust me. You're going to love this. I promise."

He presses me against the door moving his head into my neck and runs his nose along my jaw.

I sob harder and tears now flow down my face.

"Please—" I plead more knowing it will fall on deaf ears.

"Stop begging." His voice becomes angry. "I hate a needy bitch." His hand reaches out and slaps me across the face—shockingly hard.

My hands automatically cover my face to protect myself against this monster.

Jason grabs the back of my hair and flings me into the middle of the room. I stumble and fall to the floor. Quickly getting my bearings back I sit up on my knees but he's already in front of me staring down at me.

"You look so lovely on your knees for me but that's not what I want right now." He pulls my hair and drags me across the room while I scream in pain. "First, I want you chained to the wall, darling. That'll be so much more appealing," he adds.

Fear courses through me as his words echo in my mind —I'll be completely helpless—at his mercy. My cries become hysterical as I continue to scream for help.

"You might want to save your throat. No one can hear you," he says, while laughing as he drops me to the floor, "Sound proof rooms. Aren't they wonderful?"

Oh, God. Oh, God.

I'm stricken by the knowledge that no one is going to save me. No one knows I'm here. No one even knows I'm with Jason.

Suddenly, all the things he could do to me in this room are becoming painfully evident. Death immediately enters my mind—*I'm going to die.* Another round of hysterical crying overwhelms me, and I can't stop.

He stops preparing the chains as he grabs the back of my hair and pulls my face to his.

"Stop crying or I'll make this a thousand times worse." His voice drips with venom.

This is the first time he seems angry and I know I don't want to see him that way again. I stop sobbing at once.

"That's better." He brushes my tear-stained face, leans down and kisses my lips. "Trust me, this will be a night you'll remember forever." He kisses my lips again. "I never disappoint." He peers into my eyes.

I close my eyes quickly. I can't look at him or I will break out crying again and I don't want to anger him anymore than he already is.

He takes my wrists and snaps a set of handcuffs on them which cause my eyes to snap open. He grabs the handcuffs in the middle and heaves them upwards which make me stand up straight. He spins me around and presses me against the wall as his whole-body crushes against mine holding me in place. He runs his hands up and down my body as I stand trembling trying to keep from crying or moving in any manner. He places a hand on my breast and squeezes making me sob which earns me another slap across the face. It happens so fast I didn't even feel myself being spun around but somehow, I'm facing him. The pain is overwhelming the instant his hand connects.

"I already warned you. Don't make me do it again." His face is so closed to mine I can feel his deep breaths across my cheek.

I squeeze my eyes shut no longer willing to look at him. My mind tries to conjure up anything besides what is happening right now. I want to be out of this room, out of this place and away from this man.

Abruptly, the pressure of his body is gone, and I fall to the ground. I hear muffled noises prompting me to open my eyes.

I see a blur of things happening all at once. There at least five men in the room now. I glance around until I finally recognize one—Leroy.

$\mathcal{I}$ make my way back to the couch and sit down. I feel a thousand times lighter after talking to Haley. Although, she didn't offer much information about Landon. In fact, she only heightened my curiosity even more.

The mystery surrounding this man has my mind working overtime. There are so many questions so much he has done that makes no sense. *Why did he invite me to be a guest at the club when he revoked my friend's membership for a month? Why did he make sure I saw my husband with his mistress? What is in this for him?*

My problem today is whether to return to the club. I want to, there's no denying that but after everything that's happened, I'm not certain it would be the smartest idea. If I'm being completely honest with myself, I'll admit that Landon has me in every possible way and deep down I know wild horses couldn't keep me away from that club—or Landon.

After I finish my internal debate I get up from the couch and make my way into the kitchen. I open the fridge, pull out a bottle of water, remove the cap and take a big gulp.

Glancing at the clock on the stove I am surprised to see the day has passed so quickly and it is almost dinnertime. Loneliness overwhelms me quickly as I realize there is no one joining me for dinner. No one is coming home. All alone, for the first time in my life, I have no one to look after. That is such a foreign feeling to me. I have no idea what to feel anymore and even worse I have no idea what to do.

I'm brought out of my developing panic attack when the phone starts ringing.

"Hello."

"Miss Shaw? It's Leroy, from the club. I hope I'm not disturbing you?" His voice, although not the one I was hoping to hear is not unwelcome either.

"No. No, I'm not busy," I answer, startled that he is calling me.

"Mr. Miller would like to extend an invitation for you to attend the club tonight. If you are not otherwise engaged?" he asks.

Landon wants me there. He really wants me there.

"Are you sure I haven't caught you at a bad time?" Leroy asks again.

"Oh… um, no you haven't caught me at a bad time. I'm sorry. I'm just surprised to hear from you," I answer, trying to hide my enthusiasm.

"So, you will accept the invitation then?"

"Yes. I think I will accept." I keep my voice as normal as possible trying not to squeal like a school girl.

"A car will be round to pick you up a seven o'clock," he states, rather than asks.

"That won't be necessary, I can drive—"

Leroy interrupts me before I can finish.

"Miss Shaw, he would like to provide transportation. He won't take no for an answer. Please, let me send the car," he pleads.

"Okay, Leroy. Send the car if you must." I smile trying hard not to laugh.

"Thank you. I'll see you tonight."

"You're welcome. I'll see you tonight." The line goes dead.

I stare at the phone for a few minutes stunned by the sudden change in plans. My thoughts run wild with several images of what might happen at the club. Then my face morphs into a smile as I realize that I will see Landon in less than three hours. Holy shit. Three hours. There is so much to do before then. I need to get ready.

Thoughts instantly go through my head. *What should I wear? What will be expected? Should I dress up, go casual? If I dress up, should I wear a dress or a pant suit?* And to top it all off I haven't even had dinner yet. Time suddenly becomes a luxury I'm running out of.

I make my way into my room and into my closet to find an outfit. Looking through my clothes it becomes painfully clear that I lack any fashion sense and can't seem to find anything appropriate to wear. After ripping most of my clothes from the closet I settle on a dress that is meant for special occasions. It is a blue, slim fitting dress that falls just above my knees and a neckline that plunges low exposing more cleavage than I would normally show but in a tasteful way.

After picking out my outfit I head into the bathroom stripping off my clothes as I go. I step into the shower and turn on the water and set it to my desired temperature.

I am anxious and can't believe Landon has arranged this evening. I do question why he didn't call himself. *Was he afraid I would say no?* As if that were a possibility. *Is this how he asks all women out?* That thought makes me uncomfortable and has me questioning exactly how many women he has been with. I mean, he's a good-looking man, rich, successful, surely there are women lined up at the door. Then there's his other secret—the hidden side of his life. *Just how many subs have there been?* That thought sends my mind into a frenzy and I must shut them all out before I make myself insane.

Stepping out of the shower, I pull a towel from the rack and dry myself off. Grabbing another towel, I place it around my head to keep my hair in place.

As I walk into my bedroom I glance at the alarm clock shocked to find I have spent the last hour in the shower. I walk over to my dresser to pick out some undergarments to wear.

That sets off another internal debate. *What do I wear? What do I think will happen tonight? Who do I think will be seeing these undergarments? Oh really, who am I kidding?* The only person I will allow to see my undergarments will be Landon. I pick out a matching black bra and panty set and then proceed to put them on. It has been six years, at least, since I had to worry about any of this stuff.

Walking back into the bathroom I take the towel off my head and begin brushing my hair out. After blow-drying it I curl the ends so that it swings around my shoulders. I brush my teeth vigorously because good personal hygiene is a must and I really hate bad breath. I put on a little makeup which consists of some eyeliner, mascara and a little lip-gloss. Staring at my reflection my stomach does flip-flops.

"Well, that's as good as it's going to get," I mumble to myself.

I go back to my bedroom where my dress is lying on the bed waiting for me. Slipping it over my head, I pull it into place over my hips and thighs. Grabbing the two pieces that are hanging over my stomach, I tie them around my neck and adjust the front of the dress around my breasts. I go to stand in front of the full-length mirror to ensure everything is in place. I turn around and grab my shoes from the closet placing them on my feet.

Walking out of my bedroom, I head for the kitchen and glance at the clock on the stove. My nerves are now in overdrive and I can't seem to calm myself down. Looking at the clock is of no help when I realize there is still thirty minutes before the car will be here. I decide to nibble on something since I haven't eaten all day and know I will be drinking. That will not be a good combination.

I look in the fridge and pull out some cheese, placing it on the cutting board. As I reach for a knife and bring it over to the cheese I notice my hands are shaking. A lot.

The tremble went unnoticed until now but it's highly visible and I can't seem to make it stop. I place the knife on the counter and run my hands up and down my thighs pleading with myself to calm down.

He's just a man. He's just a man.

This is the mantra that is on repeat in my mind. That seems to stop the trembling long enough to slice the cheese. I wrap up the remainder of the cheese placing it back in the fridge and pull out a bottle of water. Calmly—as calm as I can be—I take the bottle of water and the few slices of cheese I have managed to slice and sit down at the breakfast bar to eat.

Time moves treacherously slow yet somehow amazingly fast if that makes sense. I am dreading the arrival of the car but I'm anxiously awaiting it too. I can't get a grasp on my feelings, they're all over the place and the butterflies in my stomach are almost painful as I glance at the clock once more only to realize that it's five minutes to seven. My heart falls to my stomach and I gulp—loudly. This is it.

I get up from the counter and go to the front hall to gather my cell phone and keys, placing them all in my purse. I take a deep breath, open the front door and right there in my driveway is the same limousine that drove me home Friday night, the same Friday night that changed my world completely.

CHAPTER 31

*R*elief washes through me seeing his face. Leroy's gaze lands on me and concern is written all over his features. He glances to the floor to the side of him and I follow his line of sight to see Jason lying on the floor with a man standing over him. I realize the man is Landon.

"Get this piece of shit out of my face," Landon bellows to the other men.

"Right away. Sir." Leroy nods.

"What's the matter, Landon? Afraid she might prefer someone other than you?" Jason hisses at him, as he spits blood onto the floor.

"You wish," Landon snarls back.

"What's wrong beautiful boy, feeling a little insecure?" Jason hisses, his voice is laced with hatred as the area under is eye swells and is red from being hit.

Leroy picks him up off the floor and practically throws

him out the door to the other men who are now waiting in the hallway. Leroy turns back to Landon.

"Anything else, Sir?" he asks as he glances at me then back at Landon.

"No, that'll be all." Landon runs his hands through his hair. "Close the door on your way out." His voice is eerily calm.

I scramble off the floor to stand but remain where I am uncertain of how to approach Landon. He still hasn't looked at me and is now standing with his back to me facing the door. I wonder what is going through his mind.

"Landon…" I attempt to talk but lose my voice.

"Don't say a word," he snaps, as he places his forefinger and thumb to the bridge of his nose. "I don't want to hear it, Alexandria."

He's angry. Beyond angry but I still can't decipher if he is angry at the situation or me.

His head snaps up and he peers straight at me. "Are you so eager that you would come in here with just anyone?" he suddenly explodes.

Shock courses through my body at his sudden accusation. I open my mouth to respond but he is suddenly in front of me and places a hand over my mouth. His gaze searches mine and my eyes plead with him to understand.

He steps away from me and moves to the other side of the room again with his back to me. I need to rectify the situation and quickly. He needs to know what really happened here.

"Landon, I—I didn't," I am cut off by his yelling.

"I told you to be quiet." I immediately snap my mouth

shut. "I'm sure by now you've had time to look over all the papers in our agreement, so you know what I expect of you." He turns around to glare at me.

I'm not sure he wants me to answer. I'm not sure what to do but I know I must explain. He needs to know what really happened here tonight.

"Yes. I've read everything you gave me, but—" I'm cuts off, again.

"There is no 'but', Alexandria. You are in direct violation of our agreement and we've barely begun." In three strides he's back to stand in front of me again. "What am I to do about that? How should I deal with this?" His voice is almost a plea.

"This—isn't what—" I try to explain, but my words are all jumbled.

"It isn't what it looks like. Right?" He looks deep into my eyes. "Is that what you were going to say because I've heard that one before."

He stands glaring down at my eyes searching them. What he's searching for I have no clue, but I see a flash of something in his eyes and suddenly I'm more terrified then I've been all night. It only lasts a second but it's quite evident that he's livid.

"I warned you. I told you that these men would eat you alive." He leans in closer, giving me a death glare. "But, did you listen?"

I want to say something, try to defend myself somehow but I don't know what to say. He's right in my face fury rolling off him in waves and I have no clue how to rectify the situation.

"No. Because if you had listened to me you would not be here right now. Would you?" He steps away from me.

I stare at him dumbfounded as I try to think of the words to explain what he saw. I feel tears escaping my eyes.

"Landon, I—"

"Don't." He put his hand up to stop me. "I don't want to hear excuses." He waves his hand at me.

He's getting the wrong idea about what happened here. He thinks I came here willingly. I must set him straight and make him see the situation for what it really is. I peer at him pondering the best way to explain.

His gaze stares straight into mine and I see it again, that quick flash of lividness. An inhuman glare letting me know he's beyond angry. I'm not certain any explanation will change his mind.

"Always so eager, Miss Shaw." His gaze burns into me and those flashes in his eyes turn revengeful. "Since you're so eager and curious let's rectify that situation right now." The look in his eyes can't be right—revenge. I've done nothing to make Landon look this way.

He stalks over to me in four strides grabbing the middle of the handcuffs that are still attached to my wrists. He drags me behind him to the back of the room to the table. He walks around the side of the table with a death grip on the cuffs and stretches my arms across the table to the other side. He attaches the chain of the cuffs to a hook at the end of the table. Coming around the back of me he pulls me by waist to the opposite end of the table forcing my arms to stretch across the entire length. He pushes my shoulders down until I bend at the waist, my chest hits the table and I turn my head in time not to face plant the table top.

Panic sweeps through me as I'm half lying on this table my hands rendered useless by the cuffs. I know this will not end well. I am trembling with fear, and my mind spins still trying to come up with a way to make him see what he is doing is wrong.

"Please, Landon. Just listen to me," I beg, the pain in my face is excruciating from the two slaps I suffered at the hands of Jason.

"Listen to you. What are you going to tell me? That you didn't walk through that door of your own free will?" He steps closer placing his face next to mine on the table. "Are you going to tell me that he dragged you into this room?"

"No. But, he—" I try to answer only to be cut off by him once more.

"That's what I thought. You would do well to just remain silent during the rest of our time together." He stands up straight and walks away.

CHAPTER 32

*L*ying on the table angry rushes through me. *Why won't he let me explain? Why won't he listen?* I want—no need—him to hear me.

Before I have a chance to open my mouth, before I have time to take a breath, Landon is back with something in his hand that he is trying to put in my mouth. I try to scream in protest, but he takes the opportunity to shove a ball into my mouth and takes the two strings attached to the ball, wraps them around my head and ties them off.

"That should keep you from attempting to get out of your punishment." He walks across the room.

Punishment?

Is he kidding?

He's going to punish me for being attacked in his club. *How did this go so wrong?* When I first saw them in the room I thought for certain I'd been saved but now I'm not so sure who is more of a threat to me Jason or Landon. I watch him across the room. His back is to me as he pulls items off the wall. He to a cabinet and pulls a few more items out of it. He spins on his heels and strides across the room to stand next me. His eyes are not the same forest green, beautiful eyes I've been falling for over. Instead, they're lifeless—dead. Void of all compassion. Cold.

Landon drops all the items on the table in my line of sight. There is a short paddle, a cane, a riding crop and some sort of whip.

He reaches out to the back of my neck. He grabs the material of my dress and pulls it. My dress comes loose, and the straps fall to the table on either side of my head.

He moves to the end of the table out of my sight where my legs are. He tugs on my dress with one sharp pull and it falls down my legs to the floor.

He grabs a hold of my calf and I begin kicking my leg trying to shake off his hand. He grabs my ankle with his other hand and drags my leg to the corner of the table. My leg is restrained with a cuff attached it to the table leg. I try to kick but can't move my leg. I begin kicking with my other leg, but he quickly scoops that one up and repeats the process. The entire time I struggle against the handcuffs and kick my legs as much as possible. I think I get in a good couple of before he restrains both legs. After struggling and testing the restraints I realize it's hopeless—I'm not getting out.

I halt my resistance and lay my head on the table glancing around for Landon. I finally catch a glimpse of him walking toward a bench with my dress flung over his arm. He places it gently on the bench and strides back to me.

"How many rules have you broken this evening, Alexandria?" he asks.

I resume struggling in my restraints once more.

"This will be a lot harder if you keep struggling." He strokes my head as if I'm a dog. "Now, let's see. You came to a playroom with another man." The harshness in his tone is shocking.

I struggle more in my bounds while attempting to talk, plead, beg, but it comes out as mumbled cries.

"You ignored my direct orders in doing so." He strokes his hand down my back stopping at my lower back. "You talked back to me. You ignored me when I told you to remain silent." By this point he's clicking his tongue.

He reaches my underwear, taking a strong grip of them he rips them from my body. Terror seizes me. His hand runs along my ass. Flames shoot through my body with the touch of his hand. I am completely flabbergasted. On one hand, I'm terrified, wanting to be out of this room. On the other hand, and more horrifying is I'm becoming aroused by the touch of his hand. *How can this be happening?*

Landon's hand suddenly leaves my behind leaving my skin missing his touch. His touch made me feel better, safer. I want to throw up. Until I feel his hand slap across my butt cheek hard, leaving a stinging pain. He continues over and over, switching from one cheek to the other, over and over.

Landon moves to the side of the table where I can see him. His eyes are glossed over, face flushed, and his breathing is ragged. He picks up the paddle from the table and moves back down the table.

This is it. This is the moment when I know I'm going to get the beating of a lifetime. My body automatically begins to fight and struggle against the restraints. My arms are killing me from being stretched so long and my wrists are raw from being in the handcuffs.

The paddle comes down on my behind hard and harsh. My heart jumps into my throat and I let out a muffled cry.

Landon's voice breaks through the pain in my head.

"You will get ten strokes for each infraction. I will use each instrument on this table." He takes a deep breath. "If you make a sound, I will start again. Do you understand me, Alexandria?"

I don't move or speak.

"Nod your head yes if you understand."

I ignore him.

"Do you understand?" he yells, his anger beyond comprehension.

I shake my head yes immediately.

"Fine, then we'll begin." He moves back down the table where I can no longer see him.

I take a deep breath and hold it, bracing myself for the impact that is sure to come. And come it does. As soon as the paddle hits my right cheek the impact pushes me up the table and before I have time to recover I'm hit again.

Whack!

"You…,"

Whack!

"will…,"

Whack!

"not…,"

Whack!

"disobey...,"

Whack!

"me...,"

Whack!

"again..."

Whack! Whack! Whack!

I bite down on the gag in mouth so hard trying not to scream. My ass is on fire and I know I can't take much more. My mind twists unable to comprehend what is happening. Before I can register anything, else Landon starts again with another instrument.

This time, I hear a slight whistle noise as a gust of pain runs across the back of my thighs leaving them stinging. I take in another deep breath as I brace myself for more torture. Although, I'm certain no matter what I try nothing will make this feel better.

Landon continues to rain his terror on me in complete silence this time. I struggle not to scream every time that thing hits my body. Tears are streaming down my face and onto the table making a puddle under my face. My nose is constantly running to the point I can't stop it even when I try to sniffle making breathing difficult.

I assume he is finishes with the riding crop. I only know by process of elimination because it's missing from the table. I hear him drop it to the floor.

Landon runs his hands up and down the back of my thighs and my rear end. Somehow his hands feel cool, almost soothing, but not enough. Just as I pray for more he removes them all together and grabs the cane off the table beside my head.

Once again, I take a deep breath and hold it, hoping to ease some of the pain I know is coming my way. And, once again, holding my breath does nothing for the pain that strikes me when that small instrument connects with my lower back.

I let my breath out quickly and bite down harder on the gag that is in my mouth. When the cane strikes me, I can't help but let out a sobbing cry.

Landon stops and comes into my line of sight.

"What did I tell you?" He gazes at what I hope are pleading eyes. "I warned you that if you made a sound I would start again," He points the cane at me.

I cry harder as I peer into his eyes not at all recognizing the man standing before me. He is so different from the man I've known for the past three weeks. The look in his eyes is empty, almost evil as I stare back still sobbing. He brushes the tears off my cheek and brings his face closer to mine.

"I'm willing to overlook it. Just this once but don't let it happen again," he warns.

More tears fall down my face as Landon makes his way back down the table. The beating continues, and I struggle to hold everything in until I finally hear the cane hit the floor.

I let out a burst of air I've been holding and sigh in relief until Landon picks up the last instrument and panic courses through me again.

"We're going to have to change positions for this one,

I'm afraid." His voice is a little too casually as my mind is screaming in terror.

The cuffs fall free from my ankles and try to move my legs, but they feel like jelly. Landon walks to the other end of the table and releases the clip that is holding the handcuffs in place. He picks me up off the table by the cuffs and begins walking to the center of the room dragging me along. I stumble along barely able to remain on my feet.

Once he stops he steadies me on my feet and reaches up to clip the handcuffs to something hanging from the ceiling forcing my arms to stretch above my head. My toes barely touch the floor and my body is now aching.

I glare directly into Landon's eyes as the tears run down my face pleading with him to stop. All my attempts are ignored as he can't understand any of my muffled cries behind the ball in my mouth.

"Shhh—" He runs his fingers down my face. "It'll be over soon." He sounds so sincere, compassionate as he attempts to reassure me.

I am not reassured. When I see the bull whip in his hand I know what is coming and it brings another wave of hysteria. Landon isn't paying any attention to me as he walks around to my backside ignoring all attempts to communicate with him.

I hear the distinct whistling sound followed by the crack of the whip just before it connects my back. All the pain I felt up until this moment is nothing compared to the pain I feel now. My body shakes with convulsions under the duress. My heart is now in my throat forming a lump that makes it impossible to scream or even breathe. My mind flies though several feelings all at once. I'm scared, angry, hurt, ashamed, betrayed. You name it, I feel it all in that moment.

I hear the whistling noise again followed by another crack. My body is shaking from head to toe and when the whip lands it feels as if it's splitting me open. My back feels like a razor blade slicing me.

There's no way I'll make it through ten strikes, the pain is too enormous, but I still haven't figured out how to stop him. By the time the third strike hits, I drop my head down and get a good look at the floor where there are drops of blood falling. That's all I can manage at the sight of my own blood my mind goes into a frenzy. I begin screaming behind my gag and kicking my legs to the point I'm swinging.

Another hit by the whip sends my head forward and I'm losing all faculties. I fight harder to remain focused, but my head is spinning. Looking back at the floor I see more blood. I try to look away but it's too late, the blackness is already starting to grip me, and I can't stop it anymore.

The last thing I remember is my head falling limply against my arm and being swallowed up by darkness.

CHAPTER 33

Opening my eyes slowly, I wonder where I am. A quick glance in my near vicinity I'm blinded by silky white material and know I'm lying down on a mattress. But my question remains, where the hell am I?

I quickly close my eyes and try to concentrate on my last memories. Everything suddenly comes rushing back. All the things that happened are now flashing through my mind as tears began to fill my eyes.

I turn my head to the other side and try to get a good look around the room. What I see is the last thing I thought I would see. Right beside me is a head of dark hair.

It looks like Landon is asleep, but his position is off. I let the tears in my eyes fall as I strain to figure out what is wrong with the way he looks. His body is off the bed leaving only his head down with his eyes closed. He looks to be sleeping as if he fell asleep sitting there.

I move my hand to his hair and brush it out of the way

to get a better look at his face. Suddenly, his eyes snap open and I scream out.

"Please, don't hurt me—please." I begin to sob out of control.

Landon raises his head and stares at me with a pained expression on his face.

"I'm not going to hurt you—" he whispers. "I promise, I'm not going to hurt you." He raises his hands in a surrender move.

My body shakes uncontrollably while I sob louder.

"Shhh—" Landon reaches out to stroke my hair with his hand.

I flinch away from him as pain shoots through my back causing me to halt all movement. My crying continues.

"Don't move—please," he begs me.

"What happened?"

"You don't remember?" he asks me, in a pained voice.

My brain flashes to what I can remember, and the club comes to mind. I recall watching a demonstration, ropes I think. It was Landon's demonstration. I remember getting jealous and leaving the room to go back to the bar. The bar where I met Jason.

"Jason—"

"Yes. You went to play with Jason." There's a note of disgust in Landon's voice. "That's where I found you. In my personal playroom I might add."

What? How can that be his personal playroom? I've seen his playroom before.

"I didn't go to play with Jason," I spit out.

"What do you mean? I saw you—" he says, angered.

"I don't know what you think you saw, but you were wrong. I didn't go in that room to play with Jason. I went in that room to watch a demonstration."

"Alexandria, do you really think I'm that stupid? Leroy saw you walk into that room of your own free will." He pauses glancing into my eyes. "You were on the lower floor. There are no demonstration rooms down there, only playrooms," he continues.

"How would I know that?" I ask, angered by his denial to believe me. "And, where the hell am I?"

"You're at my house." His eyes drop to the mattress.

"Why am I at your house? Did you bring me here to torture me more?" My sobbing begins without my permission as I attempt to get up but quickly realize I can't.

"What? No—" Landon looks offended by my outburst. "What do you mean he took you there for a demonstration?" He seems confused now.

"Landon, he told me he was your college roommate and that he was going to take me to see a demonstration. When we got in that room he shut the door and locked it." My sobs come faster, and my breathing is erratic. "He—he—attacked me," I'm crying hysterically as the tears leak down my face.

"Shhh—" He runs his hand through my hair, trying to comfort me. "Shhh—I'm so sorry," he says in a whisper.

I glance at him and notice the tears threatening to escape his eyes. *He really thinks I would do that to him? He really believes I would go to that room with someone else?*

"Alexandria, can you tell me one thing?" he asks quietly, while tears run down his cheeks.

"What?" I snap at him, attempting to back away from him.

He flinches at the tone of my voice, then lets out a breath of air. "How did the two of you get in the room?" he breathes out the question, almost fearful of the answer.

"The door was open," I relay in a softer tone.

Something flashes in Landon's eyes. He springs up off the floor and is now standing staring at me but not quite at me. It's more like he is staring through me.

"Excuse me." He releases a breath of air, "I'll be back in a minute," he says, as he turns and marches out of the room.

I'm floored. What is the big deal? So, the door was open who cares? How about the rest of the story? How about the fact that Landon tortured me for being attacked in his club? How about the fact I'm now a prisoner in his home with no way out? I do have a way out. I can get up and leave.

I try to push myself up by my arms but they're too weak. I try to roll over, but my body won't co-operate. I'm not sure what is wrong with me, but I realize I'm not just walking out of here.

I turn my head to the other side of the bed and notice I have a tube attached to my arm. Following the tube, it runs to an IV bag. *How the hell did Landon get an IV in my arm? Jesus, just how bad am I?* I guess my first assessment is wrong—I'm a prisoner after all.

Landon comes back into the room and sits in a chair beside me. He no longer looks angry or confused. He looks scared—hurt even—it's hard to tell. He sits silently staring at me making me uncomfortable.

"Landon?"

"Yes?" he answers.

"How bad am I?"

He takes a deep breath letting it slip out as he pinches the bridge of his nose with his forefinger and thumb. "Lexi, I—" He pauses and runs his hand through his hair. "I hurt you pretty bad—" He pulls on his hair some more while looking at the floor.

"How bad?" I ask in a strangely calm voice that even I don't recognize.

"My father was here—he gave you something for the pain." His gaze is glued to the floor.

"How bad?"

Landon glances up with pain filled eyes.

"He had to stich up one of the wounds," he explains, as a tear escapes his eye and rolls down his cheek.

"How many?" I scream at him.

He jumps from the sound of my voice then rushes over to me attempting to take my hand. I flinch back like he's burn me.

"Don't touch me. Tell me how many."

"He put about twenty stitches and a couple staples to close up all the wounds." His head drops to the mattress.

Shock rolls over me and I am rendered speechless. *How could someone do that kind of damage? How could Landon do that to me?* I want to scream. I want to beat him with a whip. But mostly, I want to get out of his house—now.

I am brought out of my inner turmoil when I feel the bed move. Glancing Landon's way, I notice he is shaking violently and sobbing. *Jesus, does he really think I'll feel bad for him?*

His sobs grow louder, and I can feel myself caving. I don't want to. I'm angry, hurt—scared. I want to rip him a new one, but hearing his anguish is killing me. Before I know what, I am doing I reach my hand out and run it through his hair—comforting him.

"Shhh—" My voice is quiet barely a whisper. "Please don't—" Despite the anger, the betrayal I'm experiencing I also feel compassion which confuses me.

Landon raises his head and glances at me. I can see the burning in his eyes. The sorrow and pain are evident, it's like looking into his soul.

"I'm so sorry." His breath hitches and he sobs again. "I'm so, so sorry," he repeats, as he drops his head to the mattress again.

Men always say they can't handle it when a woman cries, but when a man cries it's even worse. It's harder not to feel responsible when I know I'm not. It's harder to ignore his anguish when I know I should. Harder to blame him for the situation I'm in right now.

Jason hurt me, but Landon broke me. And, as much as I want to walk out of this house and never see him again, watching him breakdown in front of me has me second guessing everything I know I should be feeling.

I continue to run my fingers through his hair. We remain that way for some time before Landon gets himself under control again.

Finally, he lifts his head from the mattress and stares into my eyes. He lifts one hand up and brushes it against my cheek as his other hand produces a phone which he drops on the mattress beside my head.

"Lexi, you have a choice to make." He pauses, as he runs his fingers down my arm. "You can choose to call the police and report me." He lowers his head hiding his eyes from me. "Or not, and we will figure out where to go from here." He lets out a shuttering breath. "The choice is yours. I'll go along with anything you want."

My gaze remains fixed on his in disbelief. *Does he really think I would call the police on him? He really thinks that?* And maybe I should. I mean, what he did is wrong on so many levels. *Can I really do that? Can I have him charged like a common criminal?* I don't think he's a criminal. *Disturbed maybe but a criminal? If I do charge him, then what?* I would have to go to court and tell everyone what happened to me and I'm not sure if I want to do that. Not that I think I can't do it because if I had to I would but I just really don't believe that Landon belongs in jail.

On the other hand, if I don't call the police and have him charged, then what? I am supposed to just go home and forget about this? Can I really do that? What will happen to him? Will he just go on as if nothing ever happened? I can't do that. I can't just walk away not knowing if he is capable of doing this to some other girl. I would never be able to live with myself if something like this happened to someone else when I could have done something to prevent it. I'm so confused.

"I'll just go—give you time to think," he says softly, as he walks to the door. He turns to glance at me once more then leaves closing the door behind him.

CHAPTER 34

*L*ogic is telling me to pick up that phone and dial 911. My brain is screaming to do it now but my heart—my heart is saying something completely different. My heart is telling me that something is very wrong here.

Yeah, he's a masochistic woman beater.

And there's my brain again trying to overpower my heart. The two battle it out for God knows how long until I begin to feel pain. It begins slowly at the tops of my shoulders and moves down my back making me whimper.

Landon kneels beside me on the floor concern etched on his face.

"Are you okay? What's wrong?" he asks, breathlessly as if he were running.

I stare at him, confused.

"You were crying out," he explains.

"I was?"

"Yes, you were. Are you, all right?" he asks again.

"I have some pain in my back—"

Landon is on his feet rushing through a door on the other side of the room before I can finish my thought. My gaze remains on the door wondering what he is doing which eases some of the pain I'm in. I'm still amazed I cried out without knowing it. I suppose weighing all my options pre-occupied me.

After a few seconds Landon returns carrying a syringe. I suddenly feel very nervous and wish I could move. He glances at me as he's walking toward me. His face falls when he sees my expression.

"It's for the pain," he states, showing me the needle.

"I don't like needles." I feel the need to explain it's the needle not him that has my face looking this way.

"Oh, don't worry, I know what I'm doing. Besides, I'm just going to put it in your IV," he says.

Relief consumes me which must have been evident to him because he gives me a half grin as he walks over to the IV and shoots the contents of the syringe into the tube.

"This is going to make you sleep." He kneels beside me. "But, I'll be here when you wake up." He smiles, while brushing the hair off my forehead.

I smile back at him or at least I think I do my body suddenly does feel like it's mine. I reach my hand out to him which he quickly grabs and squeezes lightly. My eyelids become quite heavy as I stare at him trying to keep them open.

"Sleep, love." He kisses the knuckles on my hand.

I give into the darkness that envelops me.

Fight. Fight. God damn it. Fight.

My brain is telling me to hit him as hard as I can which I do. He goes down instantly.

Run. Run as fast as you can.

My brain tells me to run as fast as I can which I do. Running to the door I frantically try to open it and as my hand reaches the doorknob I hear him behind me his voice falling over me like a black cloud.

"You didn't think you could get away that easy, did you?" he says, while laughing.

I scramble to open the door praying that by some miracle it will open because as hard as I try the handle doesn't move.

He's getting closer, his laugh becomes more sinister and I can almost feel his breath on the back of my neck.

"He won't mind if we have a little fun," he breathes into my ear.

I scream and begin flinging my arms and legs around to knock him away from me again. I try the doorknob one more time praying to anyone to let it open and it finally it does. I swing the door open and there stands my knight in shining armor... Landon.

Thank God. Thank you, God.

These words are on repeat in my head over and over the minute I see him. Standing in front of me he looks ten feet tall and glowing like an angel. As I look up at his face to thank him for saving me the expression on his face leaves me screaming in shock. He is smiling—at Jason.

I glare over at Jason who is smiling too. Horror floods me as I realize they are in on this together.

"Landon, help me," I beg.

His smile grows wider as he looks past me to Jason.

"Ahh, my beautiful boy. I've been waiting for you." Jason smiles at Landon.

I glance between the two seized by the realization that they are together.

I scream.

Two strong arms hold me down as I try to get up. My eyes snap open and I gaze around the room lost and confused. Landon's beside me holding onto me tight. He's speaking but I can't hear what he's saying.

Focusing for a moment, I glance around the room again. A dream—it was only a dream.

I stop struggling and Landon lets me go. He reaches out and brushes the hair out of my face. I still struggle to hear what he is saying.

"Shhh. It's okay. I'm here. You're okay." He strokes my face.

"Bad dream," I whisper.

"Are you okay? Any pain?" he asks.

"No, I'm fine." I take a deep breath.

"Do you—" he hesitates for a moment. "—want to talk about it?"

I look at him, not understanding.

"The dream—?" He brushes my cheek with the back of his hand, then quickly removes it. "Do you want to talk about the dream?" His face shows a moment of hope that I quickly dash.

"No."

The dream confused me for a moment, but I know it's not real. I know there is no way Landon is working with Jason. No matter what happens with us after this incident I know in my heart that Landon is not evil. Unlike Jason.

Thinking of Jason has me wondering what happened to him.

"Landon?"

"Yes." Hope settles in his features again.

"What happened to Jason?"

"Don't worry about him." Landon's voice is sharp and cold, but I ignore it.

"Well, won't I need to talk to the police or something?"

Landon takes a deep breath before he begins. "Lexi, I didn't know what really happened until you woke up. I'm sorry." He shakes his head. "I should've realized—" He run his hands through his hair. "But I didn't. Just know that Jason will never bother you again." His face reveals the pain this conversation is causing him, but his pain is not my problem.

"Landon, it's not only me that I worry about. What if he does this to someone else?"

"He won't." The pain in his features is quickly replaced by anger.

His anger makes me cringe bringing me back to the club—the playroom.

His expression immediately softens as he reaches for me again. I flinch, unwilling to let him touch me in his state of mind.

Landon pulls his hand back and pain takes over his

features once more. He pinches the bridge of his nose before letting out a sigh.

"I'm sorry. I just don't want you to worry about that. I want you to focus on getting better. Okay?" he asks, softly.

"Okay."

Not that I would let the subject of Jason disappear. I need to figure out what happen to him. But for now, I'll take Landon's advice and heal.

"Please don't be afraid of me. It breaks my heart to see you this way," he pleads.

"It's not that easy, Landon."

"I know, but please know that I will do anything for you."

There's nothing but sincerity in his tone and deep down I know this whole nightmare is one big mistake. But after my dream—nightmare, whatever you want to call it— the events in the playroom are not easy to forget.

Watching his eyes plead for forgiveness is heartbreaking. However not knowing what happened in that room and why there's no way forgiveness can be granted. Unless he's willing to explain his behavior I'm not certain he can be trusted ever again.

For now, there are more pressing matters at hand.

"Landon, how long have I been here?"

He stares for a few minutes searching my eyes for something. I know his answer must be bad by the expression on his face and his refusal to answer.

"How long?" I demand.

"It's Saturday morning," he whispers.

"What?" I yell.

I missed an entire day.

"I want to go home."

Landon remains still staring at me with pleading eyes.

"Now."

He visibly shakes at the sound of my voice. Then something crosses his features I can't quite make out.

"You—can't."

"Excuse me? I think I can."

Who does he think he is? Does he think he can just hold me prisoner here? He already offered to let me call the police. *Did he change his mind?* That must be it. He must have changed his mind. *What now? What is his plan? What is he going to do with me?* My heart begins beating wildly in my chest and tears begin streaming down my face.

"Shhh." He wipes away the tears. "That's not what I meant," he says softly, still wiping my tears.

I look at him puzzled.

"You can't be home alone," he states, as if he can read my thoughts.

"Oh." All anger and anguish immediately diminish.

"If you want tomorrow I'll find around the clock care for you and you may return home. If you'd like," he offers. "Just so you know, I would rather you stay here where I can care for you." He rises from the floor and sits on the bed next to me.

Brushing the hair off my forehead, he leans down and kisses it.

"Are you hungry?" he asks.

Until he mentioned it, I hadn't even thought about

food. And suddenly, I'm famished and thirsty. I shake my head in the affirmative.

"I'll make you something and be right back." He gets up from the bed. "Just talk loudly if you need anything. I'll be able to hear you."

"Okay," I answer, as he walks out of the room.

CHAPTER 35

An entire day. I lost an entire day. Well, that says something about my life doesn't it? I've been here two days, and no one missed me. I want to cry. What I really want to do is scream but I know that will only make Landon rush back in here and that's not something I want happening right now. I need time to myself to figure out what I am going to do.

How did this happen to me? Two days I go missing from my life. *Has not one person noticed?* I guess the only person who would notice is the one person who has done this to me. Now that person wants to be the one to take care of me. I know I shouldn't allow it. I know I should make him take me home tomorrow. That is what my brain is telling me but somewhere deep down I have a feeling I'm not going to listen to my brain. Deep down I know I won't call the police on him and I know I'm not leaving his home tomorrow.

Again, I want to cry at how weak I've become. I want to

cry because I'm allowing a man to control my life again. I want to cry because I know there is no way I can walk away from him, no matter how much I want to. I don't cry. Instead, I decide it's time to get up out of this bed and start trying to get my life back.

Slowly I pull my legs to bend at the knee. It is painful, but not as bad as I thought it would be. I move them up and down to get some circulation back. I push my arms against the mattress and hoist myself into a kneeling position, biting my lip to hold the pain in. My breathing is labored, my heart pounding as I move onto all fours, trying to sit back on my heels.

With some pain I'm able to sit back against my feet. It's a start and it's also the first time I realize I'm completely naked. I pull the sheet around myself to cover up. My next goal is to stand up. I pull my feet around, so they are in front of me hanging off the bed while I sit on my rear end. Pain shoots through my back I can feel my stitches pulling but it's nothing I can't handle.

I scoot further to the edge of the bed and let my legs drop until they reach the floor. I steady myself on the edge of the mattress and brace myself on the nightstand as I slowly stand.

"What are you doing?" His voice shoots out from the other side of the room.

I ignore him and stand on my feet which is probably not a good idea since I let the sheet that is covering me up slip and it falls, pooling at my feet. I get dizzy and fall with the sheet. Fortunately, Landon catches me before I hit the floor.

He eases me back onto the bed, then stands to his full height, concern written all over his face.

"What do you think you're doing?" he asks, again.

"I just wanted to get out of this bed." I suddenly feel very exposed.

I reach forward to grab the sheet but can't reach it. Landon bends down, grabs it for me and covers me up.

"Thank you."

"Trying to get—" he mumbles as he walks away, "wants to get—wants to kill herself is more like it." He continues to mumble but I only hear certain words.

He comes back in front of me with a tray of food placing on the nightstand. He turns back to me and sighs.

"I have to check and make sure you didn't do any damage with your little stunt," he breathes out.

I just shrug as he sits on the bed next to me. I shift a little, so he can see my back. He places his fingers on my back and runs them up and down certain spots. The electricity that courses through me almost pushes the pain away. His touch ignites fire within in me and I become angry. *How does he make me feel this way, even after what he has done?* I'm ashamed knowing that the hands that caused me this damage and are now inspecting said damage, can still turn me on.

When he finishes, he places a kiss on my shoulder and I shudder.

"Sorry," he says.

I remain quiet. *What can one say in a situation such as this? Aren't abusers always sorry after the incident?* There is nothing I can say.

"Do you want to try and eat something?" he offers.

I nod my head, then scoot back on the bed and cross my legs. Covering up with the sheet I huff aggravated that I'm not dressed.

"Can I get some clothes?" I look down at my lap.

"I would, but to be honest, with the stitching it's probably better not to cover it up with anything. A shirt might rub on it and rip them out," he explains.

It makes perfect sense but I'm still not happy about sitting around in the nude all the time. I know by now I am pouting like a child but at this point who cares?

"I'll tell you what, you try and eat, and I'll find a nice big shirt of mine you can wear. Okay?" he asks with a grin.

"Thank you." I smile a little.

Landon places the tray of food in front of me and gets up off the bed and goes to another door that I assume is the bathroom. He disappears through the door leaving me to eat.

And, eat I do. He has made me the most delicious soup and sandwich I've ever eaten. I eat it all, shockingly fast, probably because it's been two days since my last meal. I'm famished, weak and the food is spectacular.

Landon returns with a t-shirt big enough for the hulk but soft as a kitten. It must be made of cashmere or angora, something like that, because it is so soft. He unhooks the IV from its bag by closing it off and unplugging it. He wraps the cord up and helps put the t-shirt over my head and down my arms.

It smells of pure Landon, which is pure heaven. If I could bottle this aroma I could make a fortune.

Unfortunately for me, the only thing it does is make my head spin and my brain function dwindle. It almost slips my mind that he owes me an explanation as to why I have a catheter in me and exactly how it got there.

Landon sits on the bed in front of me crossing his legs and mimicking my position. He looks down at his lap, then up at my face. He seems embarrassed but presses on.

"Why—" I don't know how to state my question. "— didn't you take me to the hospital?"

"Selfish reasons really." He pauses. "Lexi, I really thought you went with him." He ducks his head in shame for a moment, then looks back at me. "But, that's not why I brought you here. I wasn't trying to punish you by bringing you here. I was trying to keep myself out of jail. It was my father who convinced me to do the right thing and let you decide what you wanted to do. Although, after learning what really happened in that room, I now know the right thing to do would have been to call the police myself," he says.

"Why didn't you?"

"Because—" he pauses again searching my eyes. "I wanted it to be your choice. I've taken enough from you. I wanted to put the choices back into your hands. It's up to you. I deserve everything and anything you do to me. But just know this, from the bottom of my heart, I am sorry. More, sorry than you'll ever know," he says sincerely.

I believe him and there are so many more questions I want to ask but don't know where to begin. I start with a harmless one.

"When can I get this taken out?" I hold up the IV tube.

"Well, my father is coming in a couple of hours. And seeing as you can already stand on your own." He grins. "I'm sure he'll take it all out."

"So, your *father* knows *everything?*"

"Yes. He's very angry with me," he explains, "but, not as mad as my mother," he finishes.

"What? Exactly who else knows?" I ask, embarrassed.

"Just my father, my mother and the couple of guys at the club who were there." He looks at me judging my reaction. "But, don't worry about them, they're very discrete," he explains further. "Leroy, on the other hand, is very upset with what happened." He gazes at me, again.

"Why?"

"Because he watched you with Jason and he got the wrong impression," he answers. "When he helped me bring you home he was very angry at what I had done. He threatened to quit but I talked him out of it. Then when I told him what really happened he wanted to hunt Jason down and kill him. As did I, but I talked him out of that," he explains. "Now he just wants to know you're okay. So, I promised him that when you were up to it I would have you call him."

"I would like that."

It's not much, and it's not as if I know him well, but it's nice that someone is concerned about me.

"He doesn't trust that I haven't hurt you again. He needs reassurance. I don't blame him really. He saw me leave with you." He has the decency to glance down at the bed. "I wouldn't trust me either." He glances back up. "He also blames himself and wants to apologize to you in person."

"For what?"

"For not having more faith in you. For believing that you would go with that—" His head drops down and he doesn't finish.

"He doesn't need to apologize," I sigh. "If I saw me leaving with Jason I would have assumed the same thing."

Landon and I stare at each other for a few minutes. He is gauging my reaction to his revelations and I'm gauging his reaction to what happened that night. There's no doubt in my mind that he's remorseful but I also have no doubt there's more to his story, I just have to find out what it is.

Before I have a chance to ask anything else the doorbell rings pulling us both from our thoughts.

"That must be my father." He rises from the bed. "I'll be right back."

I sit absorbing all this new information. Knowing his father knows and his mother too is way too much. I can't imagine what they think of me—of him. And now I must sit here and allow his father to examine me. *Is it possible to die from embarrassment? Will this nightmare ever end?*

"Hello, Alexandria. I'm Landon's father, Dr. Miller. I'm here to check you over. Is that okay with you?" His voice is as soft as a whisper and full of concern.

"Yes, that's fine Dr. Miller. As long as you're going to take this tube out of me." I hold up my hand with the needle stuck in it.

"You can call me, Carter." He grins the same grin that his son uses on many occasions. The resemblance is uncanny. Their features are identical except Landon is dark haired with grey eyes, his father has blond hair with blue eyes. Dr. Miller makes his way to the bed.

"You can call me, Lexi. It's a pleasure to meet you." I extend my hand.

He shakes it with a small smile toying at his lip. The moment passes, and he gets right to business. He removes the IV, then he checks my vitals and looks over my stitches. When he finishes he sits on the bed in front of me and lets out a breath. He gazes into my eyes for a moment and I stare back. His eyes are very telling and let me know he has lots to say, but he seems uncertain.

"You know, Lexi. Landon is my son and I love him with all of my heart, but what he's doing here is wrong," he sighs.

I have no clue what to say. He's right, this is so wrong.

"I understand he gave you the choice what to do next?" he asks.

"Yes, he did."

"I would quite understand if you were to call the police on him. And you have every right to do so. I've already made myself clear to Landon on this issue. But—" he pauses and gazes at me, pleading. "—I've never seen my son like this before."

I'm confused. *Is he trying to tell me to call the police or not?*

"Landon has never—ever missed a day of work. He's never cared for anyone in his home before. And he has never introduced me to anyone he is dating. I'm not trying to persuade you one way or the other. I just wanted you to have all the facts. I think you're good for my son. He cares about you and is willing to do whatever it takes to fix this. I know that won't be simple, and there is no easy fix for this. But I'm just trying to say—" He pauses to think for the right words.

I reach over and place my hand on his. "I know what you are trying to say. And it's okay. You don't have to say it. I understand. You're his father and you want to protect him."

"Yes and no. I want to protect him, sure. But I also want him to realize what he's done here. I also want you to realize what you do for him."

"He does realize what he's done. And I'm not sure what I'll do from here. But know this, I won't do anything rash. I'll give it a great deal of consideration."

"Thank you. That's all my wife and I can ask." He gets up from the bed.

Landon picks that moment to walk back in the room.

"How's everything going? How's our patient?" he asks.

He sounds so young and concerned.

"She's doing well. You've done an excellent job. She should heal beautifully," Dr. Miller says to his son. "Are you still putting the lotion on?" he asks, raising an eyebrow.

Landon looks slightly uncomfortable moving from one foot to the other. I sit there wondering what the good doctor is talking about.

"Yes. Four times a day. Just as the doctor prescribed," he says with a smile.

"Good. My job is done here for today." He turns back to me and raises his hand. "Lexi, it's been a pleasure. I wish the circumstances were different, but I hope to see you again. Soon," he says.

I shake his hand. "Thank you. That would be nice."

"Landon. See your old man to the door." He turns to Landon and they head for the door of the room.

"Just a sec, Dad," Landon calls out to him and he turns to look at me.

I offer one word. "Lotion?"

"I'll explain when I come back," Landon says, with an embarrassed smile on his face.

I can feel the blush from head to toe at the thought of Landon putting lotion on me four times a day. My only wish now is that I was awake to enjoy it. Sick puppy, I know. *What kind of woman wants the man who beat her putting lotion on her?* A sick one, I tell ya.

After a few minutes Landon comes back into the room and joins me on the bed.

"The lotion is to help lessen the scars. I only put it on the stitches. I swear." He holds up his hands and crosses his heart. "I would rather you be awake when I touch you in other places," he mumbles under his breath.

I'm glad I'm already blushing. No need for him to know his touch still has that effect on me.

"I need to ask you something, but I'm afraid you'll get angry for me asking," I blurt out.

"Ask me anything."

"Why?" I lower my head.

"I was jealous," he simply states, a little too quickly for my liking.

"Landon, come on. This—" I gesture to my back. "—this is not simple jealousy," I plead. "Tell me why?"

Landon becomes very uncomfortable and starts

running both hands through his hair. He pinches the bridge of his noise and sighs. He opens his mouth a few times to say something but immediately shuts it.

With the level of stress rising in the room, I want to take it back. I want to take away his anxiety and when I am just about to tell him to forget about it—he begins to speak.

CHAPTER 36

*T*he air in the room shifts, leaving me with a sense of longing as the words begin to pour from Landon's lips.

"Jason and I were college roommates. We were really close my first year. We were always together. Did everything together, went everywhere together. He was fast becoming my best friend, until—" He pauses as a look comes over his face that I can't decipher.

Landon looks far away as sadness crosses his expression. With an audible sigh he continues. "I really liked him and in the beginning of our friendship he was exciting. He always had somewhere to go and something to do. I spent a lot of my time studying but he dragged me away from that. Making me go out and have fun. At first it was thrilling, and I really enjoyed myself. But after a while that was all he wanted to do. The problem with that was my courses were very demanding. I couldn't keep up with him and my workload. So eventually, I stopped hanging out with him." Landon pauses again looking as if he is a million miles away.

I sit as still as a statue on the bed willing him to continue. There is a lot more to this story and I want to hear it all.

He takes a deep breath and continues. "For about a month I refused to go anywhere choosing to stay home and study, get myself back on course. He would ask me every weekend to go out, but I wouldn't because the schoolwork was kicking my butt. I had to stay on top of it. During that time Jason started changing. Nothing obvious at first but enough that he wasn't the same person I moved in with. He would leave Friday nights and not come back until Sunday. He would get calls during the week and run off to God knows where. When I asked him about it he would say come with me sometime and find out for yourself. He was very cryptic about anything he was doing outside of school."

I glance up at Landon who is suddenly very quiet. His face is etched with sorrow and pain as if remembering something he didn't want to. He shakes his head returning my gaze.

"One night when I couldn't take the mystery anymore I decided to go with him. It was a Friday night, so I thought what the heck? I was dying to know what he'd been doing. As we drove through town Jason remained quiet. He wouldn't tell me where we were going or what we'd be doing. He pulled the car over in front of a house and turned the engine off. He turned his whole body toward me and spoke for the first time since we left the apartment." Landon takes another deep breath.

"He said to me 'don't judge and keep an open mind'. I had no idea what he was talking about and asked him to clarify, but he simply turned, opened the door and got out. I sat, stunned by his words for a moment and watched as he rounded the car and waited on the sidewalk for me. I got out of the car and walked up beside him as he turned and headed for the house. When we got to the door, he knocked. The door opened to a huge guy who greeted us. Jason looked at the man, said the word 'green', and the man stepped aside to let us in. I kept wondering what the hell was going on but still I said nothing and followed behind Jason as he walked through the house like he owned it. We finally came to the living room where there were a lot of people. At first, I thought it was just another party and wondered what the big deal was, but as I looked around more closely I noticed that this wasn't your typical college party. There were people everywhere, dressed oddly. In fact, some of them weren't dressed or barely had anything on at all." Landon smirks up at me.

"Let's just say I've seen strip clubs with more clothed people than the people in that room. The more I looked around the more nervous I became. This wasn't my scene and I didn't think Jason would be into something like that, either. Jason must have seen something by the expression on my face because he quickly pulled me into the kitchen and got a large glass of alcohol. I think I swallowed the entire glass in one gulp." Landon chuckles as he says this.

"Anyways, he started to tell me to calm down, pull my

shit together. He really seemed nervous at this point, so I tried to relax. Then he began explaining everything to me. He told me how these people like to live this lifestyle, how they took it very seriously. He made it sound so intriguing and before I knew what was happening he pulled me into a room where there was a woman on her knees on the floor with her head down and no clothes on. I was shocked. Jason moved around the room doing—I don't even know what because I couldn't take my eyes off the woman on the floor. She didn't look up when we came in. In fact, she didn't move a muscle at all. Next thing I know Jason was at her side petting her like she's dog, telling her how good she was. I'm sure my mouth fell open at this point but still couldn't seem to take my eyes off her. I kept wondering who she was and why she was on the floor.

"Jason tapped her on the shoulder and she stood up. She still hadn't looked up from the floor. He leaned into her and whispered something in her ear that I couldn't hear. She turned around and headed to a table in the corner of the room. She climbed up onto the table and laid down on her back. Jason went up beside her, ran his fingers through her hair and down her arm. He pulled a handkerchief out of his back pocket placed it over her eyes and tied it around the back of her head. He pulled her arms over her head and tied them with rope securing them to the leg of the table. He did the same thing to her legs too. I was paralyzed in shock as I watched everything happen."

I look down at my lap for a moment realizing that this was Landon's first experience in BDSM and from the sounds of his story it doesn't end well. Taking a deep breath, I look at Landon's eyes and give him an encouraging look to continue.

"Jason walked over to the wall and pulled something down. He walked back to the woman who was now strapped to the table and began striking her with the object in his hand."

Landon tenses up and begins running his hands through his hair. I reach up and grab one of his hands, giving it a squeeze. He looks into my eyes and lets out a long breath.

"I crossed the room in three strides and was just about to start yelling when I noticed the woman on the table practically writhing. I froze on the spot and watched as Jason continued what he was doing. After a few minutes, the woman was begging to cum. I couldn't believe my eyes or ears. None of it made sense to me but for some reason I couldn't look away. Jason turned to me and asked if I wanted to try. I'm sure I looked at him like he was insane, but he just laughed and handed me the object. After a few instructions he told me to try it. At first, I didn't want to, so I was gentle, but he pushed me to hit her harder and I did. When I looked up at the woman she was breathing heavily and seemed to enjoy it, so I continued. It felt so wrong but so right. I was torn and confused—that wasn't how I was raised, and I had a hard time processing what was happening and why. I'm not sure how long I hit her for before she was begging me to cum again. Jason warned her using a stern tone not to beg again and then smirked at me. I felt bad for the woman. She was pleading, and writhing and I knew she couldn't wait much longer. But I also felt powerful."

That word catches my attention and I look down at my lap again. So that is the reason he's so interested in this lifestyle. He wants to feel powerful. *I know he loves control but how sick is that?* My heart stops and my breath labored just hearing Landon's words. And I know, in that moment, I can never be what he wants. I can never give him that kind of power over me, especially now. My heart aches knowing the truth.

Landon puts his finger under my chin and lifts my head to look into my eyes.

"Powerful, yes. But wrong. It still felt wrong somehow. Jason leaned in close to my ear and whispered, 'make her cum', so that only I could hear. He handed me a vibrator and stepped back to watch. I looked at the vibrator in my hand for a moment, then turned back to the woman on the table. It didn't feel right to use another object on her, so I threw it on the floor. I walked closer to the table and started running my hands up and down her thighs. She was struggling in the restrains, so I moved to the end of the table and untied her legs rubbing her ankles that had red rings around them. I moved my hands back up her legs to her thighs again. Her breath hitched, and it seemed like she was still struggling. Jason told her she could vocalize at will. I looked at him—stunned. He walked over to me, patted me on the back and told me to do whatever I wanted to do with her. Then he left the room."

Landon looks over at me and I return his stare for a long while. I can't believe this was how he was introduced to the lifestyle. It's hard to wrap my brain around the story he's sharing. *How could Jason just give him a woman like that? Did he not have any respect for women at all?* After what he did to me, I guess not.

"Anyways, after Jason left I just stood and stared at her on the table. She didn't move for the first few minutes but then she started pleading with me again. This time she was calling me 'sir' and begging for release. I went to her and pulled the blindfold off her face. She was surprised to see me at first and glanced around the room, but then she fixed her pleading gaze on me—waiting. Her face was flushed, and I could tell what she needed— badly. I untied her wrists and rubbed the red circles around them, then pulled her off the table. She immediately fell to the floor at my feet and bowed her head. I was stunned and didn't know what to do at first until I remembered how Jason spoke to her. I told her to get up, lean over the table and hold the edge at the other side. She moved quickly no hesitation at all. I undid my jeans, pushed them down along with my boxers and moved in behind her. One swift push and I was inside her. My mind was racing thinking how unbelievable this was. I'd never experienced anything like that before. Don't get me wrong, I'd been with plenty of women, but never one as open as this. I mean, for Christ's sake, I didn't even know her name."

Landon glances at me with disgust written all over his face. I don't know what to say or do. I don't think anything I say will help, so I remain quiet.

"When I failed to move she let out a moan, which got me going. I moved slowly in and out of her but apparently that was not enough for her because she started telling me to go faster and harder. The next thing I know I'm slamming into her so hard the table's moving with each thrust. It felt amazing to me, like nothing I'd ever felt before and didn't even consider what it felt like to her. I just kept going as fast and hard as I could. When I was ready to release, I realized I hadn't used a condom and pulled out of her, coming all over her back. She screamed in pleasure as it spilled all over her and once again I was shocked. She turned around and dropped to her knees so quickly I had no idea what she was doing. She leaned forward pulling me into her mouth and began cleaning me up. I reached down, pushed her off me, did up my pants and left the room quickly to look for Jason. I don't even know if she got her release or not."

Landon's eyes are pleading with me to understand but I'm failing miserably. I can't figure out how he could do that, especially with someone he didn't even know.

"I waited for Jason at his car and he finally came out a couple of hours later. We didn't say a word to each other the entire way home. I was too stunned and didn't know what to say. Once we finally reached our apartment I laid into him telling him exactly what I thought of the whole night. He sat me down and explained the whole lifestyle to me. He told me that everyone was there of their own free will and that they all wanted to be there. He told me to think about it some more and when I'd made up my mind whether to be involved or not we'd talk again.

"For the next week it was all I could think about. I couldn't get it out of my head. I couldn't get her out of my head. I couldn't understand why she would want to do something like that. I knew for my part it was a turn on and to be quite frank, I'd never been harder in my life with her strapped to that table begging me for release. Like I said—powerful. But for her I didn't see the appeal. I mean, who wants to be treated like a dog? The next weekend I decided to go back. I needed answers that Jason couldn't give me. So, I told him I wanted to try again, and we went back together.

"This time I stayed in the living room while he wandered off. I watched the people in the room and spotted a man who had a sub with him and seemed to respect her. I watched him for a while and he was very good to her, so I approached him. His name was Gary. He was nice and took me under his wing, so to speak. Over time, he taught me everything I needed to know about being a good Dom. He found me some subs to train with. I did that for a couple of months, until he was satisfied I was good enough to have my own sub. He told me he would be on the lookout for a sub that would suit my needs. In the meantime, I'd play at his house or clubs that he knew because the circles that Jason ran in weren't the best for this type of lifestyle. It was amazing I had even met Gary because he didn't usually frequent the house where Jason had taken me. He believed that this lifestyle should be given freely, and that house was a pay to play house. That was the first I knew of that or else I would have never returned. Jason left that part out."

Landon appears embarrassed almost flustered confessing that part. I had no idea places such as that existed, but I suppose if people were willing to pay for sex why not this? No wonder that woman didn't care who was in the room with her—she was paid not to care.

"After a couple of months and a lot of no's later, Jason got upset with me that I would no longer indulge his lifestyle. He wanted me to hang out with him and became jealous of my relationship with Gary. I kept telling him that I wouldn't go to that house knowing I had to pay. I had no reason to, but he wouldn't let it go. He became very competitive with me and frequented the places I was hanging out in order to compete. He wanted the best-looking sub he could find. He always tried and steal the ones I played with. He was becoming quite belligerent and I was starting to want nothing to do with him. I finally moved out of our apartment and broke off all contact with him. I haven't spoken to him since then."

Landon's gaze falls to the mattress as he shakes his head.

I sit more confused than ever not understanding what this story has to do with what happened at his club.

"Landon? What does any of this have to do with me?"

"Everything, don't you see—?" He takes a large breath. "He went after you to hurt me. He went after you to try and get one over on me—again. This is his childish game and he loves to play. I'm sorry that you were involved, but this is not the first time he's tried to take a sub away from me. Although, this is the first time he went to such extremes with a woman. He's never tried to force himself on any one of my subs before. I'm sorry I didn't realize what really happened but like I said he's done this before," Landon explains.

"So why do you allow him to attend your club?"

"Because, as I've said he was never dangerous to anyone before. I never minded the competition. It never bothered me. He could have any sub of mine that I've trained if she's willing to go to him. I would advise against it, of course, because he's not the nicest man but I'm not in the habit of keeping women held captive, despite the current situation. I told you before I only train. I haven't had a sub of my own for years. But rest assured, he will never step foot in my club again. That will never happen." Landon growls.

"So, what now?"

"I don't know. I suppose that's up to you. What do you want to do? Would you like me to bring you a phone?"

"No."

We sit in silence for a few minutes. I allow everything he told me to sink in, but I'm still unsure if I can ever trust him again. His story still doesn't satisfy me, and I know there is something he is holding back, it's written all over him. I also know—thanks to my investigator—that he disappeared for five years after his first year of college. Surely, that has something to do with Jason and the world he introduced Landon to? His story doesn't end there. Now I need to decide if I want to stick around long enough to find out the rest of the story.

Silence fills the space around us to the point of being uncomfortable. He doesn't know what to say and I certainly have no idea either. After the uncomfortable silence stretches on he excuses himself for the night.

"Get some sleep. We'll talk more in the morning." He rises from the bed and walks to the door.

"Goodnight, Landon."

"Goodnight, Lexi." He plasters a forced smile across his features then turns and exits the room.

I sit on the bed for a while, wondering what the rest of his story could be. With all the information I have I know whatever happened to him has to be bad.

It's these thoughts filling my head that have me tossing and turning all night. Every time I close my eyes to fall asleep different scenarios play out. It's all becomes unnerving and I recognize the need to leave this house to think clearly.

With all the information weighing heavily on my mind I turn my head to the clock on the nightstand to see its 1:00 am. With a sigh, I fall back onto my pillow, cursing myself for not being able to turn off my brain.

The silence of the house and the thoughts running around my head are starting to give me a headache.

CHAPTER 37

J'm suddenly jolted from my self-induced haze by an inhuman scream. The blood hurtling scream has me jumping from the bed in one quick motion forgetting instantly about the pain in my back.

I step toward the door closer to where the screaming is coming from. I fling open the bedroom door and step into the hallway looking up and down the narrow space for the source of the sound. The terrifying screams never cease, and it quickly becomes apparent they are emanating from the room directly across from mine. Sneaking across the hall I stand in front of the closed door wondering what I should do. Gathering enough courage, I push the door open and investigate the dark room.

Immediately I see Landon thrashing around on the bed —screaming. He appears as if he's in the fight of his life as he kicks and screams. The blankets and sheets are twisted around his legs. From this distance, I can't tell if he is awake or asleep, so I move in for a closer look.

Stepping to the side of the bed, I notice his eyes are open and it looks like he is truly fighting someone. I freeze not knowing what to do for him. My brain starts shouting at me to talk to him.

"Landon?" I use the softest tone I can muster in my current state.

Landon's movements slow a bit but he's still screaming.

"Landon? Shhh—it's okay. Shhh—" I say, in a soft tone as if I am talking to a small child.

Landon's screams stop, and he falls flat against the mattress. His eyes close and his breathing begins to calm.

Thinking he will be okay, I start to back away from the bed towards the door. Five steps are all I get before he sits up and starts screaming again.

My heart slams into my chest as the words tumble from his mouth.

"Please stop—I'll do anything—please. Just stop—"

I have no idea what or who he is pleading with, but his voice is enough to pull me to him. Before I can register what is happening, I'm on the bed climbing up to him and encasing him in my arms.

"Shhh. It's okay, Landon. You're safe. I'm here—nothing's going to happen," I repeat the words over and over as I stroke his hair and rub my hands up and down his back.

We remain in this position for a few minutes before Landon drops back to the bed taking me with him. I lay there for a few more minutes listening to his breathing return to normal.

When it seems like he's fine, I wait a little while longer wondering what I should do. In the end, I decide that falling asleep in his bed is not the best idea and begin to extract myself from him, but he just pulls me closer and tighter to him.

I struggle to break free of his grasp, but his grip on me is strong. Finally, I relax and let the tension around me fade away.

CHAPTER 38

A sudden jolt of the bed wakes me. It takes a few seconds to figure out where I am before opening my eyes.

The night comes seeping back as I focus on the room around me. The clearing of a throat brings my attention to Landon, who is pressed back against the headboard starting at me in confusion.

"What are you doing in here?" he asks, in a shocked tone, accusation loud and clear.

"Well, I wasn't trying to molest you, if that's what you're implying," I snap back.

Landon's face crumbles as he stares into my eyes, trying to figure out what is going on. Staring back, I try to gauge his reaction. His face flashes confusion, anger and then regret. Seeing this last emotion prompts me to explain the situation.

"I heard you screaming last night and came in here to see if you were okay." I glance up at him.

His eyebrow's rise, almost to his hairline.

"When I saw you, I realized you were still sleeping and must've been having a nightmare. So, I called your name, but you wouldn't wake up. I had to climb on the bed to reach you and shake you awake. As soon as I touched you, you through your arms around me and pulled me to lie down with you. You stopped shaking and screaming so I stayed here for a few minutes to make sure you were settled. When I tried to leave, you wouldn't let me go. Your hold was too tight, and I couldn't break free. I didn't want to wake you again. After a while, I guess—I just fell asleep." I finish my rambling and peek up at Landon who seems a million miles away. I wonder briefly if he has heard a word I've said when he suddenly starts mumbling, words that are hard to make out as he runs his hands through his hair.

"Unbelievable—this time. I can't believe—" His face flashes to mine quickly and he stops mumbling. "I'm sorry. For you know—" he says, as his face softens a bit. "Shit—"

"Landon," I begin, but am cut off by his rambling.

A flash of concern takes over his expression as he moves slightly closer to me.

"Did I hurt you?" He twists his head to glance at my back.

"No, I'm okay."

Relief overtakes his features. In this moment, I know how truly concerned he is about me and what he's done.

"Thank you for staying with me," he says, so softly I almost miss it.

Suddenly his face hardens, and his eyes look far away. My body begins to tense after seeing this expression from him one time before. This is an expression I never want to see again.

Fear overtakes me as I begin to back off the bed—slowly. Landon doesn't move a muscle for several minutes as I make my way to the door. I get half way there before his head snaps in my direction. I hold my breath wondering if I should make a run for it or remain where I am. Deciding to confront him my voice comes out in barely a whisper.

"Landon? Are you okay?"

His glare remains on me, but his mind is far away. Not knowing what to do I take two more steps towards the door.

"Landon?"

His eyes come into focus and he shakes his head.

"Yeah. Yeah, I'm fine." He takes a deep breath and continues. "I think it's time to get you home. How are you feeling?"

What the hell was that?

Home. *He is trying to get rid of me? Why?* I quickly think back over the last few minutes to figure out what I said or did that made him suddenly want me gone. I can't figure it out. As I glance at his face I realize he's waiting for an answer.

"I'm good. I should be able to handle things on my own now," I reply weakly, as I start my retreat out of the room.

"Well then—let's go and see about getting you home," he says, with a little too much enthusiasm as he climbs out of the bed and begins to walk toward me.

I slither out the door and back across the hall to my

room. *My room? What am I thinking?* This isn't my room. Hell, this isn't even my house. Disappointment courses through me at the thought of returning home. It's not that I don't like my house, it's more the thought of being alone. Alone. Again. No. I can't think this way, especially after what he's done. Alone would be much better than forgiving him. He's not the person I imagined him to be. His actions —unforgivable.

Right?

CHAPTER 39

When I enter the bedroom, I glance around for a moment before realizing nothing in this room belongs to me. Everything, including the t-shirt I'm wearing belongs to Landon. I wonder what happened to my dress, shoes, everything I had with me two nights ago. I stand for a few more minutes before Landon enters the room, his face dropping to a frown as he looks at me.

"What's wrong?" he asks.

"I—um. I—"

"You what?"

"I don't have anything to wear home," I whisper.

"What do you mean? You have a closet full of clothes in there." He points toward the walk-in closet. "Surely you can find something in there to wear home?" He looks at me astonished.

"What do you mean there's a closet full of my clothes in there?" I ask, angered at the thought that he broke into my home and took my clothes.

He remains still with an embarrassed look on his face.

"Did you break into my house, Landon?"

"What? No, of course not," he responds, as he moves over to the closet door and swings it open. "I bought you clothes for the club and our—" He glances my way. "—arrangement. Leroy brought them over yesterday." He waves his arm at the closet like it the most natural thing in the world.

"Landon. Those clothes belong to you."

"No, they now belong to you. What would I possibly do with them? They were bought specifically for you."

"I can't accept them. They're too much...," I try to explain but am immediately cut off before I can finish.

"Of course, you can accept them." He walks up to me, puts his finger under my chin, lifting my head and gazing into my eyes. "Besides, even if I wanted to return them, I can't," he says softly.

Several arguments run through my mind but I'm unable to rebuff before Landon continues.

"All right, that's settled. I will have my housekeeper pack up everything and have it delivered to your house this afternoon. Now, find something to wear while I go and make sure breakfast is ready." He lets go of my face and moves toward the door. "Don't take too long," he says on his way out the door, leaving no room for argument.

I stand still wondering what just happened. Landon has a way of making you do things you wouldn't normally do. I'm not sure how he does it, but it always leaves me stunned. Knowing that I must be downstairs within a few minutes, I make my way to the closet and pull out a simple outfit of jeans and a t-shirt. After I change, I make my way to the bathroom to see what I need to do to make myself look presentable.

Looking in the mirror I begin by washing my face and decide the simplest solution for my hair is a ponytail because until I have a shower and wash it my hair will be useless.

Leaving the bedroom, I walk down the hall realizing that this is the first time I have been in this house. I have no idea where I am going.

Assuming the kitchen is on the main floor, I head for the staircase, taking in my surroundings as I move along. There are six other doors, excluding Landon's bedroom and the guest room I stayed in. The extravagance of Landon's home is not shocking, and I really want to explore more but decide this would be an inappropriate time to do so. It's also considered bad etiquette to roam someone's personal property without permission. It's at times like these when I hate my mother's teachings of manners and behavior. Its times like these I wish I were more like Haley—a snoop.

Arriving at the bottom of the stairs, I'm met by Landon.

"I thought you got lost. I forgot you haven't been given the tour," he says, rather sheepishly.

"Almost. You have a very impressive house," I remain on the bottom step to stand in front of him.

"Well, let's go. Breakfast is ready," he says, as he turns on his heel and begins to walk away.

I follow along, almost offended that he didn't offer to

give me a tour before remembering the true reason for my stay here.

Walking into the kitchen is like entering a chef's wet dream. The room is huge, the focal point a center island with a beautiful granite top. A vast number of cupboards all beautiful cherry wood takes up three of the walls. The left wall houses floor to ceiling cupboards, which awaken my curiosity. My desire to open them and discover the treasures inside is overwhelming. Lengthways on the right wall is an industrial size gas stove with a stainless-steel ventilation hood hovering above it. Along the back wall are twin industrial size stainless steel sinks. A huge bay window hovers above the sinks providing a glorious view of the back yard. Everything is in pristine condition and outfitted with modern equipment. Not a thing out of place.

At the stove is a tiny woman standing with her back to us as she cooks. When she hears us enter she spins around to glance our way. She's an older woman in her fifties, perhaps sixties. She's short—even shorter than me—but only by an inch or two. She is a pudgy woman with a round face, grey hair and sporting an apron just like any grandmother would when they were baking. She is wearing a big old friendly smile as she greets us.

"Morning, Mr. Miller."

"Morning, Mrs. Howard. How are you this morning?"

"I'm good. Very good," she replies, still smiling as though she's in on some joke I'm not privy to. "Come have a seat. Breakfast is ready." She waves us over to a table that is already set for two.

I remain still completely astonished by the fact there is

another person in the house. Dozens of questions are running ramped through my mind. The obvious one being how much she knows about me? Does she know the reason I am here? My face begins heating up and my body starts trembling with embarrassment. It's bad enough that Landon's parents know what he's done to me, does his housekeeper/maid, whatever she is, have to know, too?

Suddenly, I feel a hand on the small of my back and breath in my ear.

"She knows nothing," Landon whispers to me in reassurance.

My body relaxes immediately, whether from his touch or his words I can't be certain. The effect he has on me is indescribable and becoming to annoying. My feelings for him are growing rapidly, while he appears unaffected. It's appalling. How can I allow him such power over me after what happened?

I'm not stupid or ignorant. Hell, I'm not even desperate. I just got separated for Christ's sake. *What the hell is the matter with me?*

The pressure on my lower back increases just missing my wounds like a reminder of what Landon is capable of. It should make me pause. It should make me want to run screaming from this house, but I don't. Instead, I allow him to push me towards the table and take a seat as Landon's voice breaks through my trance.

"What would you like, love?" he asks softly.

My gaze snaps to his so I can assess his expression. He simply peers at me waiting for my response. I glance down at all the food on the table seeing enough to feed a small army. An assortment of eggs, bacon, toast, along with pancakes and waffles are on display waiting for takers. Seeing the amount of food in front of me I wonder if anyone else may be here. As the panic in me begins to swell I peer back to the two place settings available. My heart rate returns to normal when I realize it will only be the two of us.

"I'll have pancakes, please," I reply.

Landon picks up a plate, fills it with pancakes and places it in front of me. Then he reaches for the syrup and places that in front of me, too.

I can't stop staring at him, stunned that he's used that term of endearment again. It may have gone unnoticed by him, but it hasn't gone undetected by Mrs. Howard, who is currently staring at us with amused expression on her face, as Landon takes his seat.

"You two make such a nice couple," she comments.

Landon stiffens in his seat, a mixture of emotions filters across his face. Anger and confusion are front and center before he puts his mask back in place.

I remain still as a statue waiting for him to freak out, but he doesn't. He simply reaches for a couple of slices of bacon and places them on his plate before turning to looking me square in the eye.

"Would you like coffee or juice?" He completely dismisses Mr. Howard's comment.

"Um. Coffee, please." I pick up the syrup and begin preparing my meal.

It occurs to me that I haven't known Landon very long. I don't even know how he takes his coffee—if he even drinks coffee. *How can I have such strong feelings for someone I don't even know? Is it just his looks? Am I one of those women who gets totally lost in a good-looking guy? Am I that shallow?*

I peek up at him trying to determine if I'm really that shallow. There's no denying he's a Greek God. He is the most beautiful man I've ever seen, if you can call a man beautiful. I find it hard to believe my feelings are all about his looks. Landon is more than his looks—he's the total package. He's a well-respected businessman. He's confident, charming and charismatic. He's sexy, dominating, but not arrogant in the least. He must have women falling at his feet that would submit to him. Heck, I bet most of them would marry him given the opportunity.

None of that that appeals to me. What appeals to me are the things I don't know. The things that make him the man he is. He's like a puzzle I need to figure out. A mystery I need to solve. He has a vulnerability to him that I'm certain not too many people have seen. I have and can't help but think he needs me. I'm just not sure what he needs from me—yet.

Because of my staring, Landon returns my glare concern etched in his features.

"Is everything okay?" he asks.

"Yes. Sure. Sorry." I begin eating.

I can feel his gaze burning a hole in the side of my head but don't know what to say. I continue eating hoping he'll start eating too.

A few seconds later, Landon returns to his food. We are silent throughout the rest of our meal.

Once we finish, Landon stands and presents his hand to

me. I place my hand in his and follow as he walks of the kitchen and through the hall to the front door. I'm a little disappointed there will be no tour of his home. I'm sure it's amazing but I know now is not the appropriate time. I wonder if there'll ever be an opportunity.

Landon opens the front door and ushers me outside without a word.

CHAPTER 40

Sitting in the driveway is a big black car with Lawrence standing next to the rear door. I assume he's waiting for me which is even more aggravating knowing that I'm being tossed out—without warning.

Landon pulls me down the front steps to the car as Lawrence opens the door for me. I move to get in but get pulled back by Landon's grasp on my hand.

"Give us a moment, Lawrence," he says, his commanding tone making a reappearance.

"Yes, sir," Lawrence answers, as he returns to the driver's door of the car.

Landon turns me to face him placing his hand on my cheek. I hold my breath waiting to see what he is going to do or say.

"Lexi," his soft voice return.

I wait for him to continue but he just stares into my eyes for a couple of seconds making me uncomfortable. He moves his hand to brush the hair off my face.

"Are you sure you're going to be okay?"

"Um—" I stumble to answer. He doesn't seem like he wants me to go. It's such a difference from waking up this morning and I'm not sure how to answer. "Yeah, I'll be fine. Don't worry, Landon." I try to reassure him.

"But, I do worry. I still feel—"

I cut him off by placing a finger on his lips.

"Stop. It's over now. Let's not dwell on it anymore. Okay?"

"Okay. But if you need anything—" he begins, but I cut him off again.

"Yeah. Yeah. I know, call," I laugh because he's told me this a thousand times already. "You have to stop. It's time to go back to our lives."

"You're right. I guess, I'll see you around."

His statement makes it seem like we will never see each other again.

I panic. *What if I don't ever see him again? What if this is the last time we're together?*

"What?" he asks, clearly reading my confused expression.

Before I can stop myself, before I can think rationally about anything I may say or do, words fly out of my mouth without thought.

"I'll see you Friday night?" I ask, or state, it's hard to decipher.

Landon seems just as surprised by my statement as I am. He searches my eyes, for what I have no idea, but he must find an answer.

I stand like a deer caught in headlights afraid he will see

doubt, fright, desperation all the things that are currently running through me.

"Yeah, sure. Until Friday, then." He raises my hand to his lips, pressing a soft kiss to the back of it. "Good bye, Alexandria." He sounds so final.

"Bye, Landon." I step away from him and get into the car. Landon closes the door behind me.

I watch out the window as the car moves along the long driveway until I can no longer see him. My head falls back against the headrest and remains there until we pull into my driveway.

CHAPTER 41

*A*lone. That's what I've become. Alone.

Since leaving Landon's house I've been alone and don't like it. My mind won't stop thinking about all that's happened since I met him. I left my husband. I've started a new and strange lifestyle. I've been attacked and beaten.

Where did I go wrong? How did I end up here? I know I wanted more out of life. My life had become boring, but really have I asked for all of this? Perhaps I did. Maybe asking for a little excitement was just asking for too much.

Now I have a decision to make and it's one I'm not prepared for. I can go back to my boring, stagnate existence, or I can return to the club and see where things stand between us.

When he said goodbye to me yesterday it seemed so final. He acted as if I would never see him again and given everything that happened the thought of never seeing him again is disturbing.

Can we move past this? Is it possible to move forward?

I need to see him to know for sure. Waiting until Friday is not an option. I want to—no need—to make certain I'm welcome on Friday night. And the only way to do that is to see him beforehand.

I could call him and ask him to come over, but I'd rather not have such a formal meeting. His club is a better place to address the situation. Turning up at the club one night this week will catch him off guard, but it will give me an honest reaction, one I can hopefully gauge.

The ringing of my doorbell pulls me from my thoughts. I make my way to the front door and throw it open to see a blond man dressed in a suit standing on my porch with a smile on his face.

"Can I help you?"

"Are you, Alexandria Shaw?" the man asks.

"Yes. And you are?" I question, wondering how he knows my name.

"Agent Johnson. I'm an agent with the Federal Bureau of Investigations, Ma'am." The man—Agent Johnson—holds out his hand for me to shake while his other hand holds his badge up for me to see.

I stare at it for a moment, while my brain to catches up to the conversation. FBI?

"May I come in and talk with you for a moment?" the agent asks politely.

"Umm. Sure. Please, come in." Completely stunned, I gesture for him to follow me.

I walk down the hallway towards the living room hoping that Agent Johnson is following because I've suddenly lost the ability to speak. Several things are running through my mind simultaneously. *What is he doing here? What does he want? Does this have anything to do with David?*

That's probably it. David's a lawyer after all, perhaps it's one of his cases. While these thoughts are rolling through my mind, I realize we have been standing in the living room for a bit too long.

"Please, have a seat, Agent Johnson," I offer.

"Thank you, Ma'am," he says, as he sits down in the armchair and puts his briefcase on the coffee table, popping it open. He reaches inside, pulls out a file folder, closes the briefcase and places the file on top.

I sit down on the couch as he begins to speak.

"I'm going to get straight to the point, Mrs. Shaw." He opens the file, pulls a few items out and places them on the table in front of me. "Do you recognize any of these men?" he asks, bluntly.

I stare at him for a second then glance over the photographs in front of me. To my surprise I recognize three out of the five photos. My mind races even more. *What the hell is going on here? Who is this guy, and why does he have these pictures?* I don't know what to say or do, so I say the first thing that comes to mind.

"Could I see your identification again? Please?"

He had flashed his badge at the door but after seeing these photos I want a better look. I also want to stall because I feel uncertain what I should tell this man.

"Sure." he pulls his badge out of his pocket and holds it out for me to see.

"Thank you." I look it over and it seems very legit. "What is all this about, Agent Johnson?" I ask, already knowing I wouldn't get a straight answer.

"I'm involved in an investigation that concerns these men." He points to the pictures. "That's all I'm at liberty to say." He bows his head.

I return my attention to the photos attempting to buy more time, still unsure what to divulge. What I really want to know is what kind of investigation he's involved in.

"Why are you coming to me? How do I fit into all of this?"

"Ma'am. We've been watching this man—" he points to one of the photos. A photo of Jason to be precise. "—for a while now. He was seen coming out of a club downtown two weeks ago Friday. We continued to follow him closely and he led us here," he says, as matter of fact.

"This man was at my house two weeks ago?" I repeat, absolutely stunned by his revelation.

"Yes. He parked his car out front and disappeared around the back of your house. He didn't reappear for several hours." He pauses, looking at me before continuing. "Do you know who this man is?" he asks, concern evident in his voice.

"No. I don't know who he is. Should I be concerned? What type of investigation are you running on him, err, them?" I ask, pointing to the photos.

"I can't say, Ma'am. But yes, you should be concerned. This man was in your backyard for several hours without your knowledge. I would be concerned." The frankness in his tone is unnerving.

"Are you telling me that I'm not safe in my own home? Is that what you're saying here?" I'm a minute away from freaking out.

"No, there is no need for you to worry about him, Ma'am."

"Well, which is it, Agent? Should I be afraid of this man or not? I would appreciate a straight answer," I command.

"Ma'am, there's no need to fear this man." He pauses, takes a deep breath, "He's dead," he states.

Dead? What does he mean dead? My eyes flicker back to the photo of Jason. That can't be. It just can't be. My mind is racing and I'm one step from a panic attack. I sit silent, staring at the photographs in fear of glancing at the Agent because my face will say a lot more than I want it to. I'm clueless as to what I should say or how to respond. *Why is this Agent here? What the hell is going on? Should I tell him what I know?* He should know everything. He's the FBI. I should be able to trust him, but I don't. Something about all of this isn't right.

Agent Johnson's voice interrupts my thoughts.

"Ma'am are you sure you don't recognize any of these men?" he repeats.

"No. I'm sorry, but I don't," I glance at the Agent to gauge his reaction.

He knows I'm lying. I know it's written all over his face. As I've stated on more than one occasion my lying skills are horrendous. I'm in shock and can't think straight. I want to know what's going on and why this Agent has photographs of Landon, Jason and the short, black haired man from Landon's club. I also know this Agent will offer no answers, so neither will I. He needs to leave. I want him out of my house.

"Well, thank you for your time." He gathers up the photos, places them back in his briefcase and snaps it closed, the snap rings throughout the room with a finality. "Sorry to bother you and as I've said don't be concerned about that man." He stands and begins making his way to the front door.

I follow along still stunned by all the information.

"Thanks again." He turns around and holds his hand out to me.

I reach out to shake his hand, but he grabs my wrist and pulls me to him—a little too close for my comfort.

He stares straight into my eyes as he speaks with conviction. "Ma'am, if there's ever anything you want to tell me call the number on this card." He places the card into my palm. "I'm only here to help." He turns and walks out the front door.

Following him outside, I watch as he strolls down the front walkway just as another car pulls into my driveway. I continue to watch the Agent as he steps off the curb and goes across the street to his car.

He turns before getting into his car and stares in the direction of my visitor. I follow his gaze.

Standing next to his car, looking at the Agent is Landon. The two of them stare at each other for a moment, before Landon turns and heads in my direction.

I focus back on the Agent who raises an eyebrow at me. Now he knows I was lying, for sure.

I quickly return my attention back to Landon who is now making his way up my steps.

"What are you doing here?"

"Who was that?" he questions.

"Oh, just some sales guy," I lie, again.

I turn toward the house to avoid his eyes, knowing he will see right through my fib. "Why are you here?" I ask again, while opening the door and heading inside.

Landon follows close behind.

"I forgot to give you the lotion for your back," he states, as I turn around to face him. "You need to apply it two times a day."

"Oh," is the only response I can muster.

"My father says it's imperative. It will help with scarring." He rubs the back of his neck with one hand, while holding up the lotion with the other. "I pray to God he's right," he says in a whisper I'm not meant to hear. "What was the man selling?"

I stare at him for a moment stunned he would ask. "Um. What?" Is my lame reply.

"That man. What was he selling?" he asks again, staring at me intently.

"Oh. Ah—" I turn and head for the living room, sit on the couch avoiding his eyes once more, while another lie spills from my lips. "I don't know. I told him I wasn't interested before he started his speech." I can't believe how easily the lie pours from my lips. Perhaps, I'm getting better at this.

Landon remains standing his eyes never leaving mine.

"Lexi are you okay?" he asks, concern lacing his tone.

No. No I'm not okay. Shit. *Should I tell him? How can I? What do I say?* Yeah, everything is fine, that man is an FBI Agent, here investigating. He has photos of you, Jason and the creepy man with black hair from your club. Oh yeah, let's not forget that Jason has been creeping around my house for weeks and after he attacked me, he wound up dead. But yeah, everything is wonderful.

Somehow, I don't think that would be welcomed information.

"Yeah, I'm fine. Just tired is all." My eyes fall to my lap and I refuse to look at him.

"Where would you like to do this?" Landon holds up the lotion again.

I peek up at his face, bewildered. I have no idea what he is talking about.

"The lotion? Where would you like me to put this on?" he asks again slowly, as if I am stupid. "Lexi are you certain you're, all right?" he repeats, as he kneels by my side, studying my face to gauge my reaction.

"Right. The lotion." I pause to think for a moment. "The bedroom, I suppose."

Landon stares at me briefly, then rises to his full height, reaching his hand out in front of me. I grasp it like it's my life line as he pulls me from the couch.

I stare into his eyes briefly and see all the questions reflecting at me. His gaze is intent, almost breaking me and I almost reveal everything. Instead, I turn and head for my bedroom, pulling him behind me.

CHAPTER 42

*O*nce in my room, I realize I'll have to take my shirt and bra off in order for him to put the lotion on. My face begins to heat up and I'm sure it's flaming red from my thoughts about what will happen next. Letting go of Landon's hand, I head for my bathroom.

"I'll be right back," I call out as I step inside and seek refuge from his intense eyes.

Shutting the door, I spin around and look in the mirror. Red as a tomato just as I suspected. *Will I ever change? Will I always react this way when it comes to this man? Jesus, what is wrong with me?* He's being investigated by the FBI, and I'm acting like a little schoolgirl with a crush. I'm definitely twisted and in desperate need of professional help. I can almost envision the years of therapy in my future.

I remove my shirt and bra and grab a towel to wrap around myself. Opening the door to the bathroom, I freeze.

Sitting casually on my bed is mister Greek God himself.

I have imagined this, many times over the past month, but never once did I think it would be like this.

Landon glances up at me and smiles. I find it difficult to breath and my knees grow weak. Glancing back at him sitting on my bed, he takes my breath away. I yell internally at my feet to move and for once, they listen. I walk across the room to my bed.

I quickly lay flat on my stomach and wait for Landon to begin. I brace myself because I know the moment his hands touch my skin I will be done for. I press my face into the pillows hoping I won't scream when he touches me. I feel the mattress dip and can feel his body heat as he gets closer to me.

His breath drifts across my ear and cheek as he speaks softly to me.

"I'm going to have to move the towel," he whispers.

I can't look at him. I can't even breathe. So, I nod my approval instead. I feel the towel being lifted and the cool air hitting my back. The towel falls open on both sides of my body, leaving me feeling very exposed.

I hear the click of the lid and then hear Landon rubbing his hands together. The mattress dips again and he is by my side. I brace myself, as his hands touch my back with the softest of touches. He is so gentle I can barely feel him. I let out a sigh of relief as his hands still.

"Are you okay? Did I hurt you?" he asks in a panicked tone.

"No. No, I'm good. I can barely feel your hands."

His hands begin to move again with a little more pressure and the feeling is divine. He starts at the top of my back working his way down. He is very thorough. His hands are like magic, rubbing away all the stress and worry. Being surrounded by his scent is disorientating, leaving me in a daze. His warm breath on my ear tickles.

"You're going to have to stop doing that or I won't be held responsible for what I do," he states, amusement strong in his voice.

"What are you talking about?" I peek at him over my shoulder.

"The moaning," he replies, his voice still in my ear and I realize his weight is hovering over my back.

"I'm not moaning." I turn my face back into the pillow horrified because I probably was moaning.

Landon continues what he is doing and being very meticulous about it. There isn't a spot on my back that isn't thoroughly rubbed.

My wounds must be healing very well because he is causing no pain.

Just when I think he is done, he swings one leg over me and straddles my butt. I stiffen under him until I feel his lips on my shoulder. He places soft kisses to each shoulder, then pulls my arms from under my pillow and begins messaging my left arm.

I died and went to heaven. It's the only explanation for what is happening. His touch is warm, soothing and I never want him to take his hands off me. What should be a painful and uncomfortable massage has turned into the most wonderful experience of my life.

By the time he switches to my right arm the noises emanating from me are ridiculous, but I can't seem to stop.

Faster than humanly possible, Landon flips me over and is now hovering over me staring intently into my eyes. The air in the room shifts as his gaze becomes nearly black while staring at me.

I have no idea what to do. I know what I want to do. Somehow, I don't think he will appreciate me ripping his clothes off and attacking him. Immediately following that thought, lips crash against mine and before I can think his tongue is forcibly licking my lips.

Hands are frantically flying over each other as we moan and groan. All pent-up sexual tension is being released. Through a haze-induced fog, my needs are becoming agonizing, and I need to feel Landon's skin against mine.

Moving my hands to the front of him, I begin unbuttoning his shirt, starting at the collar. After the first button is undone, I move to the next one, while he moans pressing his hips into mine.

Without thought, I bring my legs around his waist and push up into him earning another delicious moan from him. Continuing my path down the front of his shirt, Landon has one hand around my neck pulling my mouth against his while he laps at me with his tongue. His other hand is around my waist pulling me impossibly closer to him.

He has my body reacting strongly as my mind completely shuts down of all thoughts, except for him. It's hard to imagine what will happen when we finally have sex.

Releasing the last button through its hole, Landon's shirt falls slightly open. I put my hands on his chest, pushing up to his shoulders to finally reveal a sliver of his chest.

Strong hands grab mine and pull them above my head. Black eyes stare directly into mine, as Landon's barge of emotions all splash across his face. His face quickly hardens into the usual mask he wears making me wonder if I even saw all the emotions he displayed.

I feel a sharp pain run down my back making me arch up and cry out in pain.

Landon pulls back looking at me one more time before mumbling a quiet, "Sorry." He jumps off the bed and quickly heads for the door, doing up his shirt as he goes.

I'm stunned as I lay exposed, panting and extremely turned on. I'm in a small amount of pain. But mostly I'm wondering what just happened?

Glancing over at Landon, he spins around, still buttoning his shirt and I catch a glimpse of a shadow on his chest, across his right nipple. My gasp has Landon glancing at me then back down at his chest. He quickly does the rest of the buttons up on his shirt as he flees my room, whispering as he goes.

"I'm so sorry. I'm sorry," he says so quiet I barely hear.

Rolling off the bed, I reach for the towel, wrapping it around myself and run after him. I make it to the door before he has a chance to make it out.

"Landon?"

He turns around with the most pained expression on his face.

"What—What happened?" I ask, quietly. "What did I do wrong?" I beg.

"Nothing," he answers dropping his head down. "I. I shouldn't have done that," he finishes, still looking down.

"Why?" I ask softly, moving closer to him. "Did you not want to? Do you not like me?" I whisper.

"No. No, that's not it at all. I like you, Lexi, I do. I just—I don't do this. I'm sorry. I have to go," he replies, but still doesn't look at me.

"Landon, look at me."

Landon peeks up at me—slowly.

"Please, tell me why?"

He stares at me looking like he is deciding something. Several emotions flicker across his face, then his mask falls firmly back into place and I know I've lost him. I know he won't tell me anything.

"I'm so sorry, Lexi. You should stay away from me. I'm no good for you." He pauses looking at the ground. His gaze snaps back to mine, shinning with determination before he speaks again. "Please, just let it go—forget about me."

Quickly, he turns, opens the door, shutting it behind himself as he walks out of my life.

I fall to the floor and like a dam that bursts the tears begin to flow. I have no idea where they come from or why I am suddenly breaking down over a man I barely know, but I can't seem to stop. My chest aches from the pounding of my heart, my mind spins with the thought of never seeing him again. That thought alone is excruciating —unbearable.

I can't understand the effect he has on me, or why he makes me feel so much. When David left my feelings weren't like this. So why on earth would Landon –a man I barely know –affect me this way?

While I am having my breakdown on the floor, the doorbell abruptly rings out. Scrambling off the floor, I swing open the door without thought, hoping its Landon and praying he's changed his mind and coming back.

A man stands with his eyebrows at the top of his hair-line staring at me like I am from another planet.

"May I help you?"

"Mrs. Shaw? Mrs. Alexandria Shaw?" the man asks hesitantly.

"Yes," I whisper.

"This is for you." The man offers me an envelope. "Could you sign here please?"

Hesitantly, I take the envelope from him and sign for it awkwardly, only now realizing I am wrapped in a towel and nothing else covering me above my waist. No wonder he is staring at me that way. I watch him turn and walk away.

"What is this?" I call out.

The man keeps walking down the driveway and onto the sidewalk. I turn and go into the house, shutting the door.

I pass the mirror in my hallway and catch a glimpse of myself. My face is red and blotchy from crying so hard. I look like death warmed over, which explains the reaction I got from the man at the door.

Turning away from my reflection I go to the living room and sit on the couch.

I open the envelope and empty its contents. Divorce

papers—great. Now I truly am alone. This day keeps getting better and better. It's not that I would ever consider taking David back but geez, I'm the one who was wronged here. *Shouldn't I be the one who initiates a divorce?*

Pathetic, that's what I am. Always sitting around waiting to see what the men in my life are going to do. Well, not anymore. I'm going to start taking control of my life. No more waiting for what others are going to do. I'm going to do what I want for a change, and what I want is —Landon.

All I have to do is figure out a way to get him.

CHAPTER 43

*I*t's been a week since I came home from Landon's, had a visit from an FBI agent and was served divorce papers. I've spent my week clearing my house of everything David. I finished piling the rest of his belongings in the garage, with his clothes and other personal stuff, I had put there previously. He is supposed to be coming to pick it all up later in the week.

I have read through the divorce documents and signed all necessary papers. Now, all there is left to do is deliver them to David's lawyer. A lawyer, with a lawyer, it's almost comical.

When my stomach growls I know some type of meal is in order. I get off the couch and move to the kitchen. After I open the fridge, I realize I haven't been to the grocery store for a while. There isn't much in there and what is doesn't appear edible.

With a grunt, I shut the door, knowing a trip is in order, a trip I really don't feel like taking. As I turn to leave the kitchen, the phone begins to ring. I reach over the breakfast bar, retrieve the phone and answer it.

"Hello."

"Lunch?" the person barks into the phone.

"Haley?" I ask, uncertain it's her.

"Of course, it's me, who else who it be?" she giggles.

She always acts like she is my only friend. Come to think of it—never mind, those thoughts will just depress me more.

"Lunch sounds great. Where and when?"

"Now. I'm at The Drake," she says quickly.

"Okay, I just have to change and I'm on my way." I tell her. "See you soon."

"Okay, but don't keep me waiting too long," she commands, and the line goes dead.

Haley can be very demanding. She's from a different upbringing than I am. Her world consists of running in the right circles, marrying the right type of man, having a life designed for the rich. Nothing like my life. It's a wonder we're still friends and in the beginning, we almost weren't.

Her parents didn't approve of me because of where I grew up, but Haley never let that bother her or change her mind about me. She's stubborn and refused to not see me. We've been best friends ever since.

I wonder what her parents would think of the establishment she introduced me to. So much for me being the bad influence on her. If they only knew the truth, Haley's father would have a stroke and her mother would chain her to the house. I smile to myself over the last thought. I can't image Haley chained to anything, but I could see her chaining someone else...

Shaking my head of thoughts, I don't want to have, I go to my room to change for lunch. Haley really has perfect timing. She always did. It's like she knows exactly what I need and when I need it. If I stop to think about it long enough, I would probably conclude she's psychic.

Before leaving, I glance at the bottle of pills on my night stand half full of the medication Landon's father prescribed me. My back is pretty much healed and from my obscured view in my three-way mirror, the issue of scaring is a non-concern. Thanks to Carter, my back should look almost as good as new, or close to it.

I haven't heard a word from Landon and I'm wondering what will happen tomorrow night. This should be the start of our new arrangement, but after everything that's happened, and the way Landon ran out of here, I'm not sure what to think.

After picking up my purse and keys from the side table in the hallway, I leave and jump into my car. The Drake is only minutes away from my house, so it isn't long before I am getting out of the car and handing my keys to the valet attendant, receiving my ticket in exchange. I wasn't kidding when I said Haley ran in rich circles. Only the best for her even if it is only lunch. She settles for nothing less.

I enter the restaurant and go straight to the hostess.

"Name?" she asks, without looking up from her seating chart.

"I'm meeting, Haley Rose?" I answer, unsure of myself, hoping she's really here.

"Ah, yes, Mrs. Shaw. Follow me." She begins walking through the dining room with me on her heels.

About two tables ahead I see Haley sitting with a smile on her face. As I approach the table she stands, and I reach out to hug her. After we break apart we both sit down.

"How are you doing?"

"Great. I'm great," she answers, with a glow on her face I've never seen before.

"Really? Great, huh? Care to elaborate?"

"What? Can't I be great?" she asks, flashing the biggest smile I've ever seen her produce. My suspicion is flying off its kilter. This is not the Haley Rose I know.

"What gives? You look like a Christmas tree all lit up," I state, smirking at her.

"Okay, okay. I can't get anything by you."

"That's right, so spill. What has you so happy?" I'm almost afraid to ask.

"I met someone," she says nonchalantly, as she sips her glass of wine.

I'm stunned and don't know what to say.

"So? You've met a lot of people."

"Yes, but this one is different, Lexi," she beams with joy.

"Different how?" I whisper. "Is he a sub?"

"Yes, but no, that's not it. He's *the* one," she answers, smiling wider.

"The one?" I contemplate that but can't think of what she means. "Which one?"

Haley sighs. "*The* one, silly. The one I'm going to marry, have kids with. My soul mate," she says, acting as if I should already know this.

"What?" I stare blankly at her waiting for the punch line. When she doesn't offer anything else, I speak again. "Are you serious?"

"As a heartbeat," she says, sipping that damn wine again.

"Haley—Oh, my God. Tell me everything," I squeal.

She squeals back, then straightens up and the flood-gates open.

"He's wonderful. So nice and funny. He's a professional football player," she says with a smirk.

"Really?"

"Yeah. I know, not my type at all," she giggles. "But let me tell you, he hasn't got an angry bone in his body. I met him at the club. Yes, he's a sub. My sub now, and we get along great. I think this is it for me. I think he's really *the one*," she says, with a gleam in her eye I've never seen before.

"That's wonderful, Haley. I'm so happy for you."

"Yeah. Well, it's not official yet. But I know it won't be long. I want you to meet him," she says.

"I want to meet him, too. Anyone who makes my friend this happy is already great in my book." I smile as wide as her.

"So, tell me what's going on with you." She waves her hand at me, turning the floor over to me.

My smile fades and I don't know where to begin.

"What's the matter, Lexi?" she asks her voice full of concern.

"David sent me divorce papers this morning."

"So, sign them and send them back. What's the problem?" she asks.

Just then, our waiter brings our plates and places them in front of us. Funny thing is, I don't remember ordering.

"I ordered for you. Hope you don't mind, but I was starving," Haley says, pointing to my plate that's filled with my favorite dish. I told you, psychic.

"Its fine, I'm starving, too." I pick up my fork and dig in.

After a few minutes of silently eating, Haley returns to our former conversation.

"What's the problem with the divorce?" she asks again.

"Nothing." I huff, as I put down my fork. "It's just—ugh. Shouldn't I be the one who initiates a divorce?"

"Does it really matter who divorces who? Don't you just want it to be over?" she asks me, always the voice of reason.

"Yeah, I suppose. It just seems wrong. I feel like it should be me who divorces him. I mean, I'm the wronged party here," I say, annoyed.

"Well, as far as I'm concerned he was a lousy husband and he should pay for the divorce because of it," she says with a smile.

When she put it that way, I feel a little better about the whole thing.

"You're right. I'm signing the papers when I get home. I want this done and over with." I give her a small smile in return and return to eating my food.

We eat in silence for a few minutes, until she begins asking the questions I have been avoiding completely, dreading this part of the conversation.

"So how are things going with Landon? How's the training going?" She quirks her eyebrow at me.

Shit. I have been so worried about her finding out what happened to me that I forgot about the training. She's going to want details. Details I can't give her. I know nothing at this point. I haven't even been through one weekend yet.

That has me wondering where I stand. *Did he just walk out of my existence or does it mean that our contract is over too?* I haven't thought about that and I can't right now because Haley is impatiently waiting for my response. *What was her question again?* Right, how it's going with Landon.

"Well—" Shit, shit. *What am I supposed to say to her?*

"Lexi, what is going on?" she asks, anger in her voice. "What the hell does, well, mean?"

She wants answers and I have none to give. I can't lie. Especially not to her. She'll know immediately if I try and lie to her. I decide to go with the truth, sort of.

"Well, we haven't started yet."

"What? Why not?" she asks, raising her eyebrow.

"Um, well there was sort of an incident at the club and we had to postpone." I offer, praying that she won't ask any more questions.

"What kind of incident?" she asks narrowing her eyes at me. "I didn't hear about anything happening at the club."

Jesus. *What should I tell her?* If I tell her the truth she'll flip out. But I can't lie. Every time I've tried to lie to her, she knew. Like I said, psychic, or perhaps she's a mind reader. Either way I'm screwed.

"Speaking of Mister Wonderful. There he is now," she says, looking across the restaurant. "Who is he with?" she asks, peering at the other side of the restaurant.

I follow her line of sight and there is Landon, in all his glory, with some redheaded woman sitting across from him.

I glance quickly, then turn back to Haley.

"I don't know, but she looks familiar."

Haley keeps staring over at them and it's making me uncomfortable.

"Stop staring."

"Why? What's your problem?" she asks, her gaze boring into mine.

"Nothing, I just don't want to attract attention."

"Why not? This isn't right. What's he doing here with her? Don't you two have a contract?" she asks quickly.

"Yes, but that only covers weekends, Haley. What he does with his private life is up to him and vice-versa."

"No, Lexi. Your contract should be exclusive. Please, tell me that you two are exclusive," she begs quietly then adds, "damn, I knew I should have read it," she says, so low I'm not sure I am supposed to hear it.

"Yes, we are exclusive. But on weekends, Haley. It doesn't matter anyways. It's over."

"What? Why? What happened?" she asks.

"I don't want to talk about it, especially not here."

"Fine, but we're not done with this conversation. Let's finish eating and get out of here. Go somewhere private to talk. Okay?"

"Fine," I answer, not really thrilled by the way this lunch is turning out, but knowing I have no other choice.

Our lunch goes along without further incident, until we're leaving. Just as we are exiting the restaurant, so are

Landon and his date, the whore. Okay, she's probably not a whore, but to me she is.

"Miss Rose, Mrs. Shaw," Landon greets us, formally.

Mrs. Shaw. *What's with that?* A week ago, it was Alexandria or Lexi. Well, two can play this game.

"Mr. Miller," I offer, coldly.

"Landon," Haley snarls his name, not bothered by the formalities. "What a pleasant surprise. It's been a while," she says, smirking at him.

Landon looks confused by Haley's informality, but responds all the same.

"Yes, it has been a quite a while, Miss Rose. How have you been?" he asks politely.

"Very well. And you? How have you been?" She growls the last word at him.

Landon quickly glances at me, but there's no way I'm getting in Haley's way.

"I've been good. What brings you two here today?" Landon directs his question straight at me, but Haley is better and answers quickly.

"We were having lunch, you know—girl talk," she whispers, covering her month with one hand.

His gaze shoots to mine. I'm frozen in place. He looks— well, he looks pissed.

"Who's your friend?" Haley hisses at him.

"Oh, pardon my manners. This is Tamara Kendall," he introduces her. "An old family friend," he adds at the last minute, glancing at me. He turns back to Tamara (the whore—family friend my ass) and introduces us.

"Tamara, this is Haley Rose and Alexandria Shaw," he says, as he points to each of us.

"Pleasure," she purrs out as she grabs Landon's arm.

It's in that moment, I realize this is the sub Landon used for his rope demonstration.

"I'm sure," Haley snarls back.

"Landon, honey, we better get going," Tamara snips. "We have to be back at your parent's house soon. We don't want to be late," she quips.

"We're fine on time, Tamara," Landon snaps back, pulling his arm from her.

The air is so thick with tension it is practically suffocating. We need to get out of here before things get worse.

I glance at Haley to see her smirking. Yep, definitely time to go.

"It was nice seeing you again, but we have to be going," I manage to squeak out.

Haley glares at me. "Yes, we do. Good seeing you again, Landon." Haley offers her prize-winning smile.

"Good to see you, again," he replies.

"I'm sure we'll be speaking soon," she says, in a tone laced with annoyance.

"I'm sure we will," Landon says, matching her tone. His tone softens as he turns to me. "Bye, Alexandria," he says.

"Bye, Landon." I turn and walk away.

Haley follows close behind, grabbing my elbow along the way. As soon as we're outside she turns me around, her face hard as stone, anger taking over her features.

I freeze when I see her face because I know what's coming.

"What the hell was that?" she whispers.

"Please, not here. Come to my house and I'll explain everything."

"Fine, but just let me know one thing, am I going to kill him?" she asks.

I shake my head and turn to give the valet attendant my ticket.

"I'll see you at my house."

CHAPTER 44

The drive to my house is short, too short, as I attempt to come up with a story to tell Haley. The truth is not something I want to reveal to her. She'll go crazy. Knowing her as well as I know her, she'll stop at nothing to make Landon pay. And making him pay is exactly where my mind is at after the little display I saw just now in that restaurant.

What was that anyway? It didn't take him long to get over what happened. Seeing him with that woman—and I use the term loosely—is overwhelming. *Was it not just a week ago that we were making out like teenagers on my bed?* Jesus, he moves fast.

My thoughts have gone in the wrong direction and before I know it, I'm pulling into my drive, with Haley right on my tail. I take a couple of deep breaths, steeling myself before exiting the car.

We walk to the door in silence while I try to think of

something to tell her. Nothing comes to me. Nothing that will explain all of this. We slip into the house, go to the living room, and sit on the couch.

Haley being who she is, starts right up.

"Spill, I want to know everything," she hisses.

"Fine, but please tell me you'll remain calm," I beg.

"I can't promise anything without full disclosure first," she states.

That isn't reassuring, and I pray I can convince her this situation isn't as dire as it sounds.

"Promise me. Please."

"Fine. I won't freak out. Okay?" she replies.

"First of all, let me get the whole story out before you say anything, all right?"

"All right, go ahead," she agrees.

I launch into my story and tell her everything, from my first visit to the club alone, right down to Landon visiting this morning.

As promised she remained quiet throughout the story.

When I finally concluded, I let out a big sigh of relief. It's as if the weight has been lifted from my shoulders. The fact that I finally have someone to talk to about all this is such a relief, until I glance up at Haley's face and can swear I see smoke rising above her. Her face is beat red, and her eyes are narrow as they glare at me.

"Why didn't you call me, immediately?" she huffs.

"I was scared."

"Scared of what?" she practically yells.

"This—your reaction. I feared what you might do."

"Do—? Do—? I'll tell you what I'm going to do," she suddenly jumps up from the couch and begins pacing, "I'm going to kill him, both of them, that's what I'm going to do," she yells again.

"No, Haley. Please, listen."

"Listen to what? Listen while you attempt to explain away Landon's actions? Listen while you twist and turn the events to make it seem like it was your fault? No." she yells louder.

I drop my head in my hands as the tears begin to fall down my face.

"I won't listen to any more of this." She pauses and glances out the window.

I pull my head up to look at her, but she has her back to me. I wait in silence for a few minutes, while she contemplates everything I told her. Suddenly, she spins around and looks at me.

"All right. Here's what we're going to do." She pauses, walks over to sit down next to me. She takes one of my hands in hers and begins again. "We're going to call the police. It's the only thing we can do," she says.

"No, we can't—I can't," I huff.

"Yes, you can. And you will. Jesus, Lexi. You were assaulted—twice. They need to pay for what they've done to you. Don't you see that?" she begs me.

"Yes, I see that with someone like Jason, but Haley, Landon's not like that. He was genuinely sorry for what happened. I can't do that to him. I just can't, and I won't," I say firmly.

She sits staring at me for a few moments.

"Let me see," she states.

"What?" I ask, bewildered.

"Let me see your back," she repeats herself.

I swallow loudly. Showing her the evidence will just make this situation worse but there's no way around it. She already knows what happened and she will not be appeased until I show her that I'm truly all right.

I turn around, so she can lift my shirt. I can feel her hands on the hem of my shirt, but she pauses for a moment and takes a deep breath before she lifts it.

She lets out an audible gasp before she starts running her fingers over what I assume are some marks avoiding the stitches.

"Jesus Christ, Lexi," she breaths out slowly. "This is really bad."

Like I don't know already. Like I'm not the one who lived through the pain.

She sits for a while longer, not saying anything or moving. I'm becoming quite concerned about what is going through her head. I knew she'd be angry, and I knew her first reaction would be to call the police, but I know I can't let her do that. I'm not sure how to convince Haley that Jason is no longer a threat to anyone without telling her the story of the FBI Agent. That's part of the story I don't want her to know. I don't want to involve her until I know exactly what I'm dealing with.

"Lexi? How are you not angry about this?" she asks, as she lowers my shirt and I spin around to face her.

"I was, Haley. I am. I'm not stupid you know. I yelled and screamed, but then we talked, and I found out a few things I didn't know. He didn't mean it. I haven't forgiven him yet, but that doesn't mean I'm stupid."

"I never said you were stupid, but I think you're wrong to forgive something like this. I think you forgave him too easily. And what did you find out anyways that would make you forgive something like this?" she asks.

"Nothing. It's not my story to tell."

She huffs in return, not buying my story at all.

"Look there are things that you don't know, things that I can't elaborate on right now. Let me just say that not all is forgiven and there is a lot more to Landon Miller than is being portrayed. That's all I can say for now. I'm sorry."

"Fine. But if anything like this happens again, I won't hesitate to chop off his balls and feed them to him for dinner. You won't be able to stop me. Understand?" she says, anger lacing her tone.

"I understand. And thank you, it's nice to have you in my corner."

"I know, better in your corner than waiting on the corner for you, huh?" she says, lightening the mood.

"That's for sure." I laugh at her, glad the tension in the air has finally lifted slightly.

"Now, what are we going to do about Mr. Landon Miller?" she asks.

I sit puzzled for a moment, not quite sure where she's going with this.

"Lexi, it's obvious you're not done with him. And from

what I saw at lunch he's far from done with you, too," she states.

I glance at her, wondering if she was at the same restaurant as I was. Clearly, he has no problem moving on. I must admit, seeing him with that other—woman, broke my heart. *Do I really mean so little to him? Can he just forget everything that has happened between us in the last month so quickly?* Well, really nothing has happened between us if I'm being honest, but I would have thought he would feel bad a little longer for his actions. The fact that he was out with another sub tells me that I'm completely wrong. Apparently, he has no problem moving on like nothing ever happened. *And, where does that leave me?* I'll tell you where that leaves me...

"How can you say that, Haley? Were you not at the same restaurant I was?"

"Yes, I was. And let me tell you, the man we saw today was enamored," she says.

"What? Did you see the stunning woman he was with? I can't compete with that. No way."

"Darling, there's no competition. She's a tramp—a whore. He would never date the likes of her," she offers.

"What do you call having lunch? And, how do you know she's all those names you called her? Do you know her?"

"Yes. Her name is Tamara Kendall, and she's a ho. Trust me, Landon Miller would not give her the time of day if her parents weren't close with his parents," she explains.

"But that still doesn't explain them having lunch together and her hanging all over him. Plus, she was his sub during his demonstration at the club that night," I add.

"She was?" Haley asks raising her eyebrow.

"Yes."

"Huh. Well, he was probably desperate and needed someone fast. The only time I've seen her sub for him is when someone else backed out, or—" She thinks for a moment. "When he doesn't have a sub. But I'm sure there is a perfectly good explanation. Trust me when I tell you nobody has respect for Tamara," she explains.

"If you say so."

"Listen, don't worry about her. Right now, we have to figure out what to do about him. You still have your membership to the club, right?" she asks.

"Yeah, I'm sure he hasn't revoked it, or at least I don't think he would." I think about that for a moment.

"No, I'm sure he hasn't. That's perfect for what I have planned," she says with a mysterious smirk on her face.

"What do you have planned?" I ask, afraid of the answer.

"Well, he wants you to forget about him, right?" she asks.

I nod my head in affirmation.

"So, you'll need to find somebody else to train you then," she states.

"What? No, no—I can't do that."

"Sure, you can, and I know the perfect guy, too," she replies, with a gleam in her eye.

"That's exactly what happened the last time. I don't want to go through that again. No, please don't."

She looks at me intently then shakes her head.

"Fine, but we have to do something, Lexi. I want to see you happy, and you're not happy. The reason I took you to the club in the first place was to make your life better, not worse. If Landon Miller makes you happy, and I'm still not convinced he can, then you have to make a play for him somehow," she blurts out.

"I'll tell you what, how about we just go to the club on tonight and have some fun. We'll just see what happens. No expectations and certainly no fixing me up with anyone." I pause and look at her. "Let's just go out and have a good time, okay?" I plead with her.

"Okay. A night out with my best friend sounds wonderful to me. Let's just forget everything for once and have a good time," she offers.

"Thank you, Haley. And by the way, I'm not wearing anything you send me. I'm going as myself, just so you know," I say, laughing at her.

"Yeah, fine. I've got to get going, but I'll call you later," she says, as she stands from the couch.

I stand along with her and we make our way to the front door. Haley stops before she opens the door and turns to me, pulling me close.

"Lexi, I really am sorry this happened to you. I never thought you would get hurt if I took you there," she says quietly.

"I know, it's not your fault. I'm okay now, really. Thanks for being such a good friend." I squeeze her before letting go.

She turns and opens the front door.

"I'll talk to you soon," she says, as she heads out the door and down the steps.

"See you later."

I stand watching as she gets in her car and backs out of the driveway, giving one last wave before she pulls away.

I shut the front door and head back into the living room and think about all the things I told her as the rest of the story unfolds in my mind. It's wrong of me to keep secrets from Haley, but most of the story is still a mystery to me. Telling her about Jason's death, Agent Johnson, his investigation and Landon's involvement doesn't seem like a wise decision at this time. It would only freak her out even more and the last thing I need is Haley storming down to Landon's club and confronting him about the situation. I also don't know if I'm in danger, but I know I don't want Haley to be in danger because of me, so until I know for certain what is happening, Haley will have to remain in the dark.

I don't even know how much he knows regarding Jason's death. I'm certain he isn't part of it, but if he knows anything at all he will be an accomplice, and I'm not sure how to deal with that. *Does he know that Jason is dead? More importantly, did he have something to do with it?* These are the questions wracking my brain since the Agent showed up on my doorstep. *Landon isn't a killer, is he?* He's a control freak and he has a lot of questionable people working at his establishment. I mean, really, Leroy appears more like a Secret Service Agent then he does a bar manager.

I also wonder about Landon's driver, too. He's a scary individual and now that I'm thinking about it his entire club reminds me of all the mafia movies I've watched on television. Everyone is so secretive. Security in that place is better than Fort Knox and what is with all the security anyways? I've been to high-class clubs before and they're nothing like his club. The security is nowhere near as tight as is at Landon's club.

Can he be a criminal?

Is that what's really going on there?

It can't be. Landon is an upstanding, well respected, businessman in this town. There's no way he can be a criminal. People would definitely know.

Flopping back down on my couch the envelope on the table is mocking me. Picking it up, I pull out all the papers and begin reading, again.

It's pretty straightforward because really, we don't have that much. The house, our own cars and some savings. According to these papers, everything will be divided equally giving me the option to buy David's portion of the house. That seems amicable to me, but it also seems too easy. Five years of marriage erased by the stroke of a pen almost like it never happened. I suppose, I should be thankful we have no children. Children always complicates divorces. I've seen enough to know that children always cause the wars in most divorces.

I put the papers back in the envelope, putting the envelope back on the table, I know I will courier it to my lawyer tomorrow. That's it. My marriage is over, and my life forever changed.

I suppose the saddest part is that I feel nothing. No sorrow, no tears, no remorse—just nothing. I'm not sure why I haven't seen it sooner, that my marriage was a farce, but I have to assume I didn't want to see it, until now. Now that it's over, I'm truly relieved that I can get on with my life. With one mess cleaned up, I can begin to concentrate on the other mess I've created.

CHAPTER 45

*A*fter getting ready, I stand patiently waiting in the hallway for Haley. My stomachs in knots, my heart is pounding, and my hands are shaking as I anticipate this evening. I can't even begin to imagine what could possibly happen and there are no scenario's playing in my mind.

I hope Landon will be happy to see me and I hope he'll want me there, but something deep down tells me that won't be the case. I have a feeling I'm setting myself up for heartache as I pray I'm wrong.

The horn blaring in my driveway pulls me from my thoughts. Grabbing my purse and keys, I head out the front door. As I walk down the driveway, I notice a car on the road a couple of houses down that looks familiar. I stand by the passenger side of Haley's car and stare at it for a moment.

I've seen that car before, but I can't remember where.

"What the hell are you doing?" Haley asks, as she leans across the front seat. "Are you coming or what?"

I investigate the open window to see her looking at me like I have two heads.

Sighing, I open the car door and get in. Haley backs out of the driveway and we pass the car in question. The windows are tinted, and I can't tell if someone is inside or not.

I look back as we pass and still can't see anything.

"What are you looking at?" Haley asks, as she looks in the rear-view mirror.

"That car back there." I point to it. "The black one, it looks familiar."

"Well yeah, it's a black sedan, there's a ton of those around," she offers as an explanation.

"No, I mean I've seen that one before, I just can't remember where." I turn to look at her. "Oh, forget it. I'm probably just being paranoid," I say, laughing.

"Okay, so what's the game plan?" Haley asks.

"Game plan?"

"You know. How you are going to win over the elusive, Mr. Miller?" she asks, glancing in my direction.

"Would you please keep your eyes on the road."

"Fine, but tell me, what are you planning?" she asks again.

"I'm not planning anything. I'm just going to go and if he's there great—if not, I don't really want to think about that."

"I've been thinking about it, and I think you should actively seek another Dom," she states.

"What? Why would I do that?" I ask her shocked she would even suggest it.

"Because, it will get his attention. Nothing like jealousy to make him realize how much he wants you," she says with a smirk.

"And what if it backfires and he doesn't care? Then what? I'm stuck with somebody I don't even want," I counter.

"Okay. What if I arranged it? If I called in a favor and have someone pretend—"

I cut her off before she could finish. "No, Haley. Thank you for the offer, but I would rather play this straight. No games—no plans. I just—I want to go and see his reaction to me being there. I want to see if I'm still welcome or not."

"Okay. We'll play it your way," she offers with a calculating look on her face.

I frown at her.

"I'm serious, I'll behave. I don't like it, but I won't do anything," she promises.

"Thank you." I smile at her. "Let's just have fun tonight. It's been so long since I've just had fun."

"Fine. Fun. I can do fun," she says, a smile spreading across her face.

Arriving at the club, we are greeted by the doorman who wishes us a good night.

Entering the room that has become so familiar to me, I take a seat on the couch and wait for Leroy to arrive. Haley sits beside me, looking rather nervous, which is out of character for her.

Before I have a chance to say anything, the door opens, and Leroy makes his appearance.

"Miss Shaw, wonderful to see you again," he says, as he comes to stand in front of me.

I rise from the couch to greet him. This has been the first time I've seen him since the incident, and I wonder what he thinks of me—of that night.

"Thank you, Leroy. It's wonderful to see you again," I say, smiling.

He grabs my hand and kisses the back of it, then looks into my eyes before speaking again.

"Everything is well?" he asks quietly.

"Yes, I'm good. Thank you for your concern, but it's not necessary," I say waving my hand at him to dismiss his worry.

"Oh, but I am—worried that is. What happened was—"

I cut him off quickly. "A misunderstanding—that's all. I'm fine. I promise," I say, smiling at him.

"Yes. I can see that, you look stunning," he offers, then turns to Haley.

"Miss Rose, you also look stunning. How have you been?" he asks.

"I've been good. How's business?" Haley returns with attitude.

"Good. Business has been good. Getting to be our busy season, you know," he rambles.

"Yes, I do," she sneers at him. "Quite the crowd you've had in here since my absence, or so I've heard," she hisses at him.

"Yes well, nothing like that will ever happen again," he says to her.

"I should hope not," she growls at him.

Things are getting very tense in the room and I need to lighten the mood quickly before we find ourselves thrown out.

"We are here to have a bit of fun tonight. Aren't we, Haley?"

She is in a staring match with Leroy, and I'm not sure she even hears me.

"Yes. We are," she finally says, glancing at me before turning back to Leroy.

"I'm sure we can accommodate you," Leroy offers.

He walks over to the hidden cabinet in the wall, pushes a few buttons and the drawer comes out. He digs around the drawer for a moment before pulling his hand out and walking back over to us. He hands me a card and one to Haley.

"Okay, there you are. You are both set, and I will see you at the end of the night," he says with a smile.

I stand there in shock. This is the first time I've been given my own card. I'm speechless. I suppose that means I am welcome after all. I turn to look at Haley, but she is still glaring at him.

"Thank you, Leroy," I offer.

"You're welcome, Miss Shaw," he says, with a small smile.

"Please, call me Lexi."

He just smiles, takes my hand again and kisses the back of it.

"Have a wonderful evening," he says, then turns and walks out of the room.

I turn to look at Haley, and she looks mad.

"He gave me my own card," I squeak.

"Well of course he did, you're a member now. It comes with the territory," she states.

"Well I guess that answers my question of whether or not I'm welcome here."

"Of course, you'd be welcome, Lexi. After what Landon did to you, you should own the damn place," she snaps. "I mean it's not like he's going to push you to do something about what happened. He's probably going to be accommodating as hell after what he did," she hisses at me.

"Thank you. That makes me feel so much better," I snap back, as I head for the door to the club.

"Lexi, that's not what I meant," she pleads with me.

I put my card in the slot and wait for the door to open. Haley comes up behind me and puts her arms around my shoulders, hugging me from behind.

"I'm sorry," she lets out a gust of air. "It's just so hard to be here and not tell someone off for what happened. Forgive me." She spins me around to look at her. "Please," she begs.

"It's okay, I forgive you."

I pull her to me for a hug. The door opens, and we go in. Haley puts her card in the next slot and the door to the elevator opens and we walk in.

Turning around, Haley pushes a button and we are on our way. I'm becoming more anxious by the minute not sure being here with Haley is such a good idea after all.

The way she was with Leroy just now and the way she was with Landon at lunch the other day, I am starting to get a bad feeling about all of this. *What if she confronts Landon? What if she says something in front of everyone?* I don't want anyone else to know. Too many people know as it is.

The elevator dings and the door opens. Haley immediately steps out into the hallway, but I hesitate.

"What's wrong?" she asks turning to face me.

"Haley, please don't do anything that'll make a scene tonight. Please," I beg her.

She moves back to stand between the elevator doors and reaches her hand out to me. I grab it immediately and walk towards her.

"I promise. I'll behave. It'll be hard, but I'll do it," she says with a small smile.

That makes me smile back. The elevator door tries to close but she pushes it back then moves out of the way, so I can get out. Once in the hallway, we head in the direction of the bar room. We walk side by side this time, enter the room and head straight to the bar.

I immediately try to get the bartender's attention and he makes his way over as soon as he spots us.

"Miss Shaw, what can I get you?" he says with a smile.

I stand staring at him like he has a third head. Thank God, Haley is in her right frame of mind.

"We'll have wine. White, please," she says.

"A white wine for the pretty lady and a cosmopolitan for Miss Shaw. Coming right up," he says, turning to go make our drinks.

Haley huffs and then turns to me. "What the hell was that? I said white wine. Where did he get—?"

I cut her off quickly. "That's exactly what I was talking about, Haley. How do they know?"

"Know what? Surely, he's served you before?" she asks, astonishment written all over her face.

"No, I've never seen him before in my life. I told you, everyone here seems to know who I am and apparently what I drink. It's weird, don't you think?"

"Yeah, it's weird all right," she says, thoughtfully.

The bartender returns with our drinks as I open my purse to retrieve my wallet.

"It's all covered, Miss Shaw," he says with a smile, and wanders back to the other end of the bar.

"See, I told you," I say to Haley, who still looks deep in thought.

I pick up my drink and pour about half of it down my throat. My stomach is still in knots, my head running through all kinds of thoughts and my nerves are shot.

Haley finally comes back to the present and looks at me.

"Okay, take it easy with the drinks tonight," she says, as she takes my glass from me and sets it on the bar. "I admit that was weird, but if we're going to find out what is going on, we need our heads tonight," she states.

"You're right." I brush the hair from my forehead.

We stand silently, and I look around the room. Inside I'm praying Landon will walk through the door. Unfortunately, that hasn't happened yet.

"He's going to show," Haley whispers to me, as she leans in close. "Quit worrying."

I'm glad she's so confident. I, on the other hand, am feeling very unsure that coming here was the right thing to do. I am starting to feel uncomfortable as the dread washes through me. Getting out of here sounds like the best idea to me and I can think of nothing else but going home to wallow in self-pity. It's time to face reality, and the reality of the situation is that Landon doesn't want me, he never wanted me and it's time to deal with that and move on.

Haley brings me out of my thoughts as she elbows me in the side.

"Ouch! What did you do that for?" I snap at her.

Her expression throws me off. She looks outraged and disgusted.

"Oh—My—God," she whispers not looking at me.

I follow her gaze to see what she is staring at. My heart drops to my stomach and I believe I stopped breathing. My prayers are finally answered as I look at the door to the room and Landon walks in.

He is sharply dressed in a gray suit that fits in all the right places as he gracefully strolls into the room, with an air of confidence that matches his style. He looks as gorgeous as ever, but there's something different about him. I can barely take my eyes off him and wish he would look my way.

"I can't believe he would do this," Haley snaps quietly beside me.

I turn to look at her again, wondering what she is mumbling about, but she's still staring at Landon. I bring my attention back to him to figure out what has her in a mood. That's when I notice the two people with Landon.

They're on either side of him and about a foot back. They're two of the most beautiful women I've ever seen. Scantily dressed with their heads bowed and their arms behind their backs, hands clasped together. Immediately, I know they're subs, but I wonder what he's doing with them. He told me he only trains subs, so perhaps he's having a training session.

I glare closer at the two women and notice one of them is Tamara. *What is he doing with her?* The saying, 'be careful what you wish for', comes to mind as I watch him walk across the room and sit in a chair.

The two women kneel on either side of him and bow their heads. Landon glances at them one at a time, then runs his hands through their hair. The touch is so loving, so tender I want to look away, but like a train wreck I can't. *Why would he do this? What is he trying to prove?*

Stunned, bewildered and hurt I stand there staring at the display that is playing out before me. My head is screaming for me to run out of this place and never come back, but my heart tells me to stay and see what he'll do next. Listening to my heart, my feet are frozen to the ground and I watch as my heart splits in two.

"Lexi?" Haley whispers to me, grabbing my arm.

I shrug her off immediately and step to the side, but my glare remains on Landon. I want him to look at me, I need to see his eyes as he spots me, but his attention remains on the women at his sides. I stand staring and waiting, for what I have no idea. Maybe, I want to torture myself.

Perhaps, I want to deny what my eyes are clearly seeing. Why I stay, and watch is beyond anything I can fathom, but I do and the next thing that happens puts my whole obsession with Landon Miller into perspective.

He leans over and gives Tamara a hand signal. She moves closer to him and reaches for his belt. As she slowly starts to unbuckle it, I can feel the tears building in my eyes. I stare straight at Landon willing him to look at me, but he keeps his eyes on Tamara. She gets his belt undone and is beginning to undo his pants.

That's all I can stand as I turn on my heel and run for the door. I run down the hallway to the elevator and push the button praying my wait wouldn't be too long. The door opens, and I rush in, pushing the button and willing the doors to close.

Once I am safely inside with the doors closed, the tears begin to spill out of my eyes. It feels like an eternity waiting for the elevator to make it to the floor I want.

Finally, the doors open, and I run out and I'm shocked to see Leroy in the room.

"Miss Shaw," Leroy says, attempting to smile.

That will not work, not tonight. I will no longer take anything from this place. All I want to do is go home, on my own. I throw my card at Leroy and head for the door.

"Miss Shaw, please," he pleads.

"Goodnight, Leroy," I shout, and open the door, running out into the alley.

"Evening, Miss Shaw," the doorman says.

I run past him and down the alley. I hear Leroy behind me yelling, but I keep going. I run out to the sidewalk and keep running down the block. There's no way I want Leroy or anyone else catching up with me.

When my feet start hurting, I slow down and glance around. I notice a cab heading down the road and flag it down. It stops in front of me and I climb in, not looking back. I tell the cab driver my address and sink back against the seat as he pulls away from the curb.

Tears stream down my face as I think about tonight's events.

How could I be so foolish?

How could I fall for a man who clearly never cared about me?

Had I not learned anything from my failing marriage?

Clearly there's something extremely wrong with me. I want to stop thinking about this. I want to go home, curl up in my bed and not think about anything ever again. But, my mind won't stop replaying the events, no matter how hard I try to stop it. *What I really want to know is what the hell is wrong with me?*

CHAPTER 46

*A*fter the cab drops me at the house, I go straight to my bedroom and put on a pair of pajamas. My intention is to crawl into bed and sleep for a week. I am so exhausted, but my mind won't stop working, so I know sleep won't come easily.

As I lay here, wishing for darkness to consume me, I hear pounding on my front door. For a moment I get scared because the pounding is forceful, but then immediately the doorbell starts ringing and I think what burglar would ring the doorbell or pound on it for that matter? Pulling back the covers, I walk to the front door and swing it open.

Standing there with her back to me, looking around the neighborhood is Haley. I should have known it would be her. I should have known she would come after me when I left the club the way I did. But to be quite honest, I had almost forgot she was with me. I ran out of there so fast, I don't remember her following me. I'm pretty sure Leroy was only ran after me.

"Haley?"

She spins around and glances at me up and down, noticing my pajamas.

"Lexi, where the hell did you run off to?" she asks, quite forcefully before pushing past me and walking into my living room.

I follow dutifully, while feeling bad for leaving her at the club without a word. That's the effect that man has on me. I forget the world around me. I forget everything when Landon is near. This must stop. This can't be healthy for me. Even my own husband never had this effect on me. *So how the hell can a man I barely know have this much power over me?*

Haley sits on the couch and watches me as I take a seat in the chair. She hasn't said anything else and is looking at me expectantly. *What is she waiting for?* Oh right, she asked me a question. *What was that again? Where did I run off to?*

"I'm so sorry, Haley. I shouldn't have run off on you like that, but I just couldn't stay," I say as the air leaves my lungs. Taking a deep breath, I peek up at her, hoping she will understand.

"I'm not mad at you, Lexi," she states. "I was worried about you after what happened. I tried to call you, but you wouldn't answer. I just had to make sure you were all right," she says smiling a little.

"I'm fine—I think." I huff a releasing breath of air. It feels like I haven't been able to breathe since I saw Landon's display earlier at the club. "I just couldn't watch him with—" I trail off, unable to finish my statement. My eyes fall to the floor, embarrassment floods my cheeks.

"Lexi?" Haley questions me, but I refuse to look at her. "Lexi look at me, please," she requests, making me feel worse.

Slowly, I lift my gaze to hers. She takes one look at my expression and sighs heavily. A moment later she is kneeling on the floor in front of me, taking my hands in hers.

"Listen to me. Everything will be okay," she says in the softest voice I've ever heard her use. "This isn't as bad as it seems," she finishes, offering me a smile.

My mind is rolling her words around my head, trying to make sense of them. *What does she mean 'it isn't as bad as it seems'? Did she not see what I did? Where was she when I was witnessing Landon's display of pornography?* I know she was standing right beside me. She had to have seen what was happening, or should I say what was about to happen before I fled the scene. *In fact, she remained there after I left, surely, she witnessed the whole event?*

"Haley, how can you say that? You were there—" I pause to take a deep breath before continuing. "You saw what was happening as plain as I did. This is worse than it seems," I say, releasing another huff in annoyance.

"Yes. I was there the whole time," she says with an angry expression on her face. "But you weren't," she finishes.

"What's that supposed to mean?"

Haley stands up and pulls me with her wrapping me in a strong hug. Pulling back, she brushes some hair off my forehead and gives me a genuine smile.

"Come here. Sit down and let me explain," she commands, while pulling me to the couch.

Bewildered, I sit on the couch staring at her with my mouth gaping open. How she intends to defend what I saw with my very own eyes I had to hear.

"Oh, Lexi, when I saw Landon come in with those two girls, especially Tammy, I was furious. I thought—" she pauses to collect herself. "I thought—Oh, I don't know what I thought, because the fury that rose in me was beyond anything I'd ever experienced before. To think that man did what he did to you and then has the nerve to show up there all casual and nonchalant. Well, I don't need to tell you that I almost went straight over to him and—well, you know. Anyways, with my head spinning and all the emotions I was feeling in that moment I stopped and really looked at what was going on," she says quietly, while staring into my eyes.

"What was going on?" I question her but continue before she could finish. "What was going on was he was about to get—"

Haley interrupts me before I have a chance to finish.

"I know. I know what it looked like. I was there too, remember? But as I stood there watching the scene unfold, I knew something wasn't right," she says, looking into my eyes again.

I'm not sure what she is trying to relay currently, but I am eager for her to continue.

"As I watched Landon's face, I noticed he was detached, like he wasn't even there. It was weird, Lexi, I'm telling you. I know this whole thing was weird because he's never done anything like that before. I've told you before that most of the time you never see him in the club with a sub, unless he's training one for someone else. To see him so open and public with two no less, I knew something wasn't right."

I stare at her in disbelief. She's really here to defend his actions, but I owe it to her to listen to what she has to say. She's not someone who would condone the actions I saw Landon taking tonight. Or even at lunch the other day.

"Haley, just get to the point please."

"I am. After you ran out, Landon pushed Tamara away," she says.

"What do you mean?"

"I mean, as soon as you were out the door, he shoved her away and his head fell into his hands," she repeats and then stares at me for a moment. "Lexi, he made sure you were gone, but I don't think he saw me there. He pushed Tamara off, put his head in his hands for a minute, then he stormed out of the room. I don't think he knows I saw everything. I don't know what it means, but I can tell you this, he did this on purpose. It was all a show for your benefit," she says, as she turns away from me. "What I'm not certain about is why?" she says, letting out a deep breath of air. "Why would he do that?" she repeats, as she turns back to me.

"I have no idea, but I'm done playing," I say, as the rage floods through me. *How dare he? Who does he think he is?* After a moment I start again. "I'm done. Finished. I can't take the game playing or the unknown anymore. I give up. If he wants me to stay away, tonight was a good plan to make that happen. I'm not going back," I say, as I stand up and go to the window.

Haley follows behind me, pausing for only a moment before wrapping her arms around me and hugging me from behind.

"Lexi are you sure that's what you want?" she asks quietly.

As the tears fall from my eyes I keep my gaze on the window as I respond.

"No, but I have no other choice, Haley," I voice, as my heart aches. "He doesn't want me," I finally admit as my shoulders start to shake and gasps of breath leave me.

"Oh, honey. I don't think that's the problem. There's something else going on," she says softly, as she squeezes me tight.

"What? What could possibly be going on?" I ask, as I try to control my anger.

Suddenly, there's a knock at the door. Quickly, I turn to look at Haley, who is looking towards the front door.

"Are you expecting someone?" she asks, slightly uptight.

"No," I reply quietly. "Who would I be expecting?" I ask with a huff, as I turn toward the door.

Haley grabs my arm before I can move.

"Sit down. I'll take care of this," she says as she walks toward the door.

I walk over and am just about to sit down when loud voices begin to filter through the room. I quickly make my way to the hallway where Haley is backing up as Leroy walks toward her.

"Get out," she yells at him, but he doesn't budge.

"Leroy?"

"Miss Waters," he says, in a quiet voice.

His use of my maiden name instead of my married one startles me.

"What are you doing here?" I say, surprised to see him.

"I had to come. Please, may I come in?" he asks politely.

"Yes." I grab Haley's arm.

We all make our way to the living room where I sit down on the couch with Haley as Leroy chooses the armchair. The silence grows to an uncomfortable level making me anxious to know why Leroy is here.

Before I can think of something to say, Haley jumps right in.

"What are you doing here?" she sneers at him.

"I came to make sure Lexi was—" he trails off as he looks me over.

"All right, Leroy. Is that what you were going to ask? If I am all right?" I voice, a little louder than necessary. His eyes widen at my tone, but he remains quiet. "No. I'm not all right, if you must know," I shout as I stand up. "I'm—it's just that—No, I'm definitely not all right, but what I really want to know is why you are here? Why did he send you here? He got what he wanted—I won't be back," I shout, as I drop back down to the couch. Haley pulls me to her and hugs me as I whisper, "I know where I'm not wanted," I say, too low for anyone to hear.

"Are you happy now?" Haley yells at Leroy. "Why don't you just leave her alone?" she demands. "Haven't you people done enough?" she growls at him.

"It was not my intention to come here and upset you

further. I was truly worried about you—" he says sincerely, but I cut him off.

"No," I yell. "No, you came here because he ordered you to. So please, just leave," I say, as I sit up and look him in the eye. "And, you can tell Landon that I'm fine and he doesn't need to worry about me. In fact, tell him to just leave me alone," I say, with a confidence I never knew I had.

Leroy sits dumbfounded for a moment, before he gathers himself together and stands up. He looks directly at me before he speaks his next words.

"I am sorry for all that has happened, Miss Waters. If there's ever anything I can do for you, please call me." He reaches into his jacket pocket, pulls out a card and hands it to me. I take it and look back up at him.

He sighs and turns on his heels towards the front door. I follow slowly behind him. When he reaches the door, he grabs the handle and hesitates for a moment before turning towards me.

"I am truly sorry," he says quietly, before opening the door.

We stand there for a moment, before I realize that he's not moving through the door. I thought maybe he was going to say more, but when I look at him again I notice his stance is different. He's stiff, resembling a statue. He begins to speak, but I've never heard that tone from him before and wonder what's wrong with him.

"What the hell do you think you're doing here?" he says, through what I assume is clenched teeth. His tone, murderous, and I'm floored.

I'm clueless as to who he is taking to, since he is blocking the door. I peek around his arm to see who is there.

Shock registers immediately when I see the odd man from the club with the jet-black hair, standing on my porch.

"Ah," the odd man says with a smile. "There's the girl I've been looking for," he says, staring right at me.

CHAPTER 47

Shock rolls over me as I stare at the strange-looking man.

"Do you know him?" Leroy hisses at me, snapping me out of my shock.

"No," I say firmly, as Leroy turns back to the man.

"What are you doing here, Alistair?" he sneers at him.

"I came to talk to the young lady. Not that it's any business of yours, Leroy," the odd man says, with a smile on his face as he glances back at me. "The name's Alistair, and it's a pleasure to make your acquaintance, Alexandria," he says, offering me his hand.

I don't move, I don't breathe as I try to figure out how he knows my name. Leroy, on the other hand, is furious as he smacks the man's hand away.

"Get out of here. You have no business being here," he snaps at him.

"Oh, I believe I do," he snaps back, and begins moving forward.

Leroy stands to his full height trying to intimidate the smaller man, but Alistair is not backing down. I stand looking between the two of them wondering what this is all about.

"What the hell is going on here?" Haley comes storming down the hall, stopping short of running me over. All three of us turn to look at her, but no one says a word. "Somebody better start talking fast or I'm calling the police," she says, waving the phone around.

"There's no need to involve the law," Alistair simply says, as we all turn back toward him. "I assure you, I have no intention of harming anybody here," he offers, as he looks at me and smiles. It's the same disturbing smile he gave me at the club on my first visit. There wasn't anything nice about it then, and there certainly isn't anything nice about it now. "If I could just have a few minutes of your time, this will all be over, and I will never bother you again," he says softly, as he keeps smiling at me.

Leroy steps in front of me before I can say a word. "You have no business here. Leave. Now," he orders.

Alistair glares at him for a moment, then turns back to me. "I hoped it wouldn't come to this," he offers, as he waves his hand in front of Leroy. "But, you leave me no other choice," he finishes, as he lets out a low whistle.

Suddenly, three huge men come from the side of my house. I instantly start to back up from the front door and step right into Haley, who hasn't budged. Turning my head to glance at her, she gives me a look of panic.

Everything seems to happen at once after that. Haley

starts dialing but doesn't get very far when a hand grabs the phone from her.

Leroy is swinging at one man, while another grabs him and restrains him.

I push Haley with my back, trying to move her down the hallway.

Alistair is watching me closely as he steps closer to us.

"Please, this is not the way I wanted this to go," he pleads with me.

I look at Leroy, who is struggling to fight two huge men. I look back at Alistair and know we are defeated.

"Stop," I shout at them all.

All at once everything stops and everyone stands where they are, looking at each other. I look Alistair in the eye.

"What do you want?" I plead.

"Just a few minutes of your time, then I'll be gone forever," he says softly.

"Fine," I say sharply.

When I turn to go into the living room, Haley glares at me like I've lost my mind. She's ready to fight, I can tell by her stance, but I don't want anything to happen to any of us.

I walk around her, determined to find out what this man wants, then get rid of him. Sitting on the couch, I wait for everyone else to come in. Before long, we are all seated in my living room. Haley, Leroy and I sit on the couch, while Alistair takes a seat in the armchair. His three goons stand close behind him.

I sit looking at my lap for a moment as I build up the confidence to face this man. As I glance up at him, he sits calmly, with a sinister smile on his face. I want to wipe that smile and his smug look into next week. Instead, I resort to a calm front of my own.

"What is it you needed my time for?" I ask confidently but am cowering on the inside.

"Well," he begins as he moves forward in the chair, placing his elbows on his knees. "You see, you have something I want, and it's only a matter of time before it's mine again. Like it should always have been," he says, smiling that evil smile.

I sit, stunned by his words. *What is he talking about? What do I have that he wants?*

"I'm sorry. I have no idea what you are talking about."

Alistair starts chuckling. "I imagine you wouldn't." He laughs a little more before turning deadly serious. "You see, you take things for granted. I know because I did for a long time too, but now I'm here to rectify that," he says, as he glares at me.

This is going nowhere fast and I need to figure out what this guy wants, and quickly. I want this pack of people out of my house.

"How will you be rectifying anything, and what role do I play in all of this?" I ask, truly curious now.

"Well, my dear. As I've already told you, I just need some of your time," he says still smiling at me in that creepy way.

I glance at Haley, who is staring at Alistair with venom in her eyes. I peek over at Leroy, he doesn't look much different than Haley, so I turn back to the man in question and he seems cool as a cucumber. He's not fazed one bit by these two starring daggers at him. In fact, he's only looking at me.

"I can see the appeal," he finally says, so softly I almost miss it.

"Appeal in what?" I ask on reflex.

"You," he simply states.

"Me...? I'm sorry I still have no idea what you are talking about," I reply, confused.

"You know, at first I thought this was all an act. But now I see you're as truly innocent as you seem," he says smiling again.

Leroy growls beside me, garnering everyone's attention.

"Leave her alone. You won't like what happens if you don't," he growls out, in a voice that has me backing away from him.

"Leroy, I understand you are under orders, but let me assure you no harm will come to the girl," he says firmly, but there's deception in his voice. "I've already gone far out of my way to ensure no more harm comes to her," he says, with a huff.

"It was you," Leroy breathes out quickly. "You killed Jason, didn't you?" he asks.

My head whips around to hear Alistair's answer.

"I take what's mine very seriously, boy. And he messed with what was mine," he says, in an agitated growl. "Now, as I know you are under orders," he glares at me while he states that. "I will let your slip go this once, but don't try my patience again. You will not like the results," he promises, with a tone of finality in his voice.

"Orders? I already knew he was ordered to come here. If that's the game your trying to play it won't work," I say in a huff. "So, if there is nothing else you want here—" I say, as I stand up to show him to the door, but his voice cuts me off.

"I will leave when I get what I came for," he snaps, letting his nice mask slip. He lowers his head for a moment, then looks back up at me—mask back in place. "Please have a seat. It won't be long now," he says softly, but in a way that has me sitting immediately.

CHAPTER 48

The room fills with a frightening silence as we wait for I don't even know what, but I know I want this over and these men out of my house. Now, I have a better picture of who this man is. He is the one who killed—or at least had someone kill Jason. And now he sits in my house as if he were an invited guest, while I'm sitting here in my pajama's, still wanting to go to bed and wallow in self-pity for a week. That was my plan before all this unfolded, but now I'm left wondering what all this is about. What I just learned I know that I'm not going to like the end-result.

Outside, I hear a car pull into the driveway, followed by the slamming of a door, and all I can think is who and what is coming now?

Everyone turns their head towards the hallway where the front door is as the silence grows thicker. I hear foot-steps leading up the porch to my front door. To my surprise, the door opens and shuts as I wait to see who enters.

Landon steps through the hallway and into the living room. Everyone, including Alistair, stands as he approaches. No one says a word. Instead, everyone is starring at Landon, while his eyes remain on Alistair.

"Landon. So good of you to join us." Alistair smiles that disturbing smile at Landon.

I stand shivering from his greeting. I look up at Landon, wondering what he is going to do. The words that pour out of his mouth stun me.

"Master," Landon says, as he bows his head.

Leroy stiffens next to me, Haley gasps, and I sink back down to the couch. The weight of his words floor me, and I can no longer stand on my own.

"My boy," Alistair breathes out a sigh of relief. "You have returned," he says smiling.

"Yes," Landon whispers, but his head remains down.

"Prove it," Alistair suddenly snaps.

Landon lifts his head and looks at him. Alistair clicks his tongue.

Leroy takes this moment to step in front of me. I grip his arm to peek around and look at Landon.

Landon's gaze remains on Alistair, and the way they're staring at one another is like they're having a private conversation.

"Now." Alistair's voice shouts in a demanding tone.

Immediately, Landon begins taking off his suit jacket.

"What's he do—" I'm cut off as Leroy spins around, covers my mouth with his hand and pleads with me to remain quiet. He moves me, so I am in front of him and we continue to watch in silence.

Landon places his suit jacket on the arm of the chair and starts undoing the buttons on his shirt. His eyes never leave Alistair, and when I glance at Alistair his gaze dances with excitement.

For the life of me, I can't figure out what is going on. *Did he really call him master? Can it be true?*

Landon shrugs his dress shirt off and in one smooth motion, he pulls his undershirt over his head. He turns to place everything on the chair, making me gasp when I see what covers his back. He has a tattoo that fills his entire back that says Property of Alistair in black bold letters.

He turns to look at Leroy when I gasp, allowing me to see the front of him. I gasp even louder seeing his chest. On his left peck, right above his nibble is the letter A. But this is no tattoo, it looks like a burn. Alistair had branded him.

My mind is racing, my heart beating as I stare at Landon's eyes, hoping he will look at me. I hope he says something—anything.

Instead, he turns back to Alistair, walks toward him until he is a foot away, drops to his knees and bows his head again. Alistair runs his hand through Landon's hair and hums appreciatively.

Alistair snaps his fingers and one of his men rushes to his side presenting him a box. Alistair opens the box and pulls out a collar. It's a thick black collar with a ring on it. It looks like it belongs on a dog. He walks around to the back of Landon and holds the collar over Landon shoulders in front of his face.

"Do you accept my collar of your own free will?" he asks.

I wait on bated breath, willing Landon to look at me. If I could just get him to look at me he would stop this. But he won't turn his head and his next words break my heart.

"Yes," he says softly. "I accept it, Master."

Alistair puts the collar around Landon's neck and clasps it into place. He grabs a handful of Landon's hair and pulls his head back holding it against his legs. Landon looks up at him.

"Oh, how I've missed you," Alistair says with relief in his voice.

Alistair leans down and kisses Landon fully on the lips. I watch in horror as he deepens the kiss with his tongue. It feels like hours have passed as I watch their make out session and Alistair make quite a show of it, rubbing his hands all over Landon and moaning more than necessary.

I don't know what to do. I want to look away but can't. I stand frozen to the spot, not believing my eyes. There is no way this is happening. *How is this happening?*

Suddenly, Alistair pulls back with a smile on his face. He walks back in front of Landon and gives him a hand signal. Landon immediately stands up, facing him. Alistair turns and pulls something else out of the box.

He shakes it out, and to my horror it's a leash. He clips it to Landon's collar with a snap. He turns to us and smiles.

"Well, it's been a pleasure, but we must be going now,"

he says, turning back to Landon. He grabs his face in his hands and speaks softly to him. "Let's go home," he sighs.

"Whatever you wish, Master," Landon answers.

Alistair pulls on the leash and Landon follows him and they head for the front door.

I can't just let him leave. I have to say something.

"Landon." I call out.

Landon stops abruptly, causing Alistair to stop. He pulls on the leash, but Landon doesn't move. I know this is my last chance. I know I must tell him before he walks out of my life forever.

"I love you," I whisper to him.

He turns, and instead of looking at me, he looks at Leroy. He gives him a sharp look and Leroy nods his head. Then Landon turns, looks at Alistair and nods his head. Alistair pulls on the leash again and lets Landon take the lead as they walk out my front door.

I collapse onto my couch as the front door shuts closed. I can't breathe, and my heart is pounding so loud I think everyone can hear it.

How could he do this to me?

What happened?

Why would he choose to be with him?

Was I really that bad?

I can't wrap my head around it. I can't figure out what happened in this room. He went with him willingly. He called him Master. *How could he do that?*

As fast as Landon walked into my life—he walked right back out.

READERS

THANK YOU, KINDLY

Wow. What a ride that was. And that ending. I know, I know, but it couldn't be helped. Did you enjoy the story? I hope so because I loved writing it.

Want to read more of Lexi's journey? The next installment takes her across the world and back in her attempts to save Landon. From what? Well, not even she's certain yet, but I promise it'll be an action packed ride. Grab *Bound Book 2*, today

Bound Book 2 - The Mystery of Landon Miller Series

If you are so inclined to leave a review I would be overjoyed to hear your thoughts. Good or bad. It helps me grow as writer and I appreciate the time people take to review.

R.M.GAUTHIER

ABOUT THE AUTHOR

Constantly writing, R.M. Gauthier is always trying to produce new material. With two series under her belt and two more on the way, she will continue to work hard in order to bring her readers more of what they love. In the meantime, you can find all her works at the follow links:

Website

www.rmgauthier.com

Join R.M Gauthier's Newsletter and receive two free stories!

http://eepurl.com/dhB5xs

ACKNOWLEDGMENTS

There are several people who help with the resources for this novel, the trailer and the advertisements. It is with a special thank you, and a shout out to each person who helped make this dream a reality.

To "Designed by Freepik," for my chapter heading designs. You can find their work here: **Freepik**

Footage for my trailer:

Unripe Content footage available here: **Unripe Content**

Mitch Martinez footage available here: **Mitch Martinez**

Cinetrove footage available here: **Cinetrove**

Music for trailer:

Ross Bugden, find his music here: **Ross Bugden**